I0687130

A WALK IN THE PARK

Natalie Kleinman

SAPERE
BOOKS

A WALK IN THE PARK

Dedicated to Elaine Everest and her love of dogs

Published by Sapere Books.

24 Trafalgar Road, Ilkley, LS29 8HH

saperebooks.com

Copyright © Natalie Kleinman, 2025

Natalie Kleinman has asserted her right to be identified as the author of this work.
All rights reserved.

No part of this publication may be reproduced, stored in any retrieval system, or transmitted, in any form, or by any means, electronic, mechanical, photocopying, recording, or otherwise, without the prior written permission of the publishers.
This book is a work of fiction. Names, characters, businesses, organisations, places and events, other than those clearly in the public domain, are either the product of the author's imagination, or are used fictitiously.
Any resemblances to actual persons, living or dead, events or locales are purely coincidental.

ISBN: 978-0-85495-651-7

CHAPTER ONE

A person would have to be mad to go out in such weather. But Daisy Shepherd knew she was mad, and in any case Oscar needed a walk and she was paid to take him. By the time they reached Greenwich Park, her jacket was soaked and rainwater was running off the end of her nose. All it needed now was...

"Whoa!" Daisy tripped over her own feet and staggered as the huge dog, still attached to his lead, attempted to give chase to a squirrel that had leapt from a tree and landed right in front of him. The squirrel, sensing danger, took off with the dog in hot pursuit, Daisy determinedly hanging on until she landed in the mud on her knees. She could already feel the bruises. Relinquishing the chase, Oscar turned his attention to Daisy. Her head was now level with his, and he chose to express his concern for her welfare by licking her face.

"It's a bit late, but thank you."

She scrambled to her feet and removed the lead from his collar, but instead of racing off again he nudged the pocket where she kept his ball.

"Oh, so now you want to play, do you?" she said, and obligingly threw it with all her might.

After their game, Daisy walked Oscar home and left him in the garden while she let herself into the house through the front and removed her dirty boots and coat. With towels at the ready, she opened the back door into the kitchen and Oscar barged past her, skidding to a halt on the tiled floor. Rubbing him down wasn't the easiest job in the world. He had a habit of rolling onto his back and demanding she rub his tummy, and a Bernese mountain dog has a lot of tummy. Daisy obliged. It was the part of the job she loved best.

"My God, you're smelly."

Oscar faced her square on. He didn't appear to have taken exception.

"Okay, it's time for your breakfast. What's Gloria left for you today? Ooh yummy. There you go then."

Daisy fed him, threw the dirty towels into the washing machine and made a token sweep of the floor, all the while keeping up a one-sided conversation until Oscar, exhausted and replete, curled up in his basket in the corner. She'd met the cleaning lady a couple of times, and Irena had told her not to bother with the cupboard doors where Oscar usually shed much of his dirt with an almighty shake.

"I used to come earlier, but there's no point. I clean the kitchen. He makes it dirty. Better to come after his walk."

Daisy often wondered what Oscar's owner Gloria did in her office all day, but she was willing to bet it didn't involve getting her hands dirty. She'd never met her husband, Arnold, though the photo in the lounge showed him to be as well-groomed as his wife. Occasionally she amused herself picturing the two of them walking Oscar at the weekends. At least she hoped they walked him. Daisy kissed the top of his wet head and said, "You're still smelly, but I love you. See you tomorrow." She smiled as she retrieved her belongings, unable to imagine either 'parent' appearing bedraggled and with an assortment of black, white and tan-coloured hairs on their clothing. How they'd ended up with such a labour-intensive dog she didn't know, but somebody groomed him, that was for sure. Daisy locked up and went home.

Once inside she enjoyed a quick shower, even though she knew her next charges were waiting for her and she'd have to do it all again later. Walking dogs had never palled in all the time she'd been doing it. She put on clean clothes and went to get George and Mildred. They were scratching at the door as she walked up the path. They weren't confined to the kitchen, but the gate across the stairs and the closed living room door prevented them from venturing beyond the hall. The wall where their leads hung was covered in scratches, bearing witness to their enthusiasm. Daisy played with them for a few minutes. They obviously came from Norfolk Terrier stock, but a bit of something else had crept in somewhere along the line. It had done them no harm.

"Okay, you two, you've had your tummies rubbed and your itches scratched. It's time to go."

At her words, they jumped up for their leads. A bit of rain wasn't going to dampen their excitement. At least George and Mildred didn't have Oscar's bulk and strength. What they did have was a launcher, which sent their ball three times as far as Daisy could have thrown it. The rain stopped as they entered the park and a few minutes later the sun put in a tentative appearance. Playing ball as they went, the trio headed for the playground where several children asked if they could stroke the dogs. Daisy knew they were less fearful of these two little ones than the lumbering Oscar, not appreciating that he wouldn't hurt a fly. However, George and Mildred were excitable and had sharp claws, so Daisy knelt down between the two to keep things under control. They were panting from their exertions and quite happy to have a fuss made of them for a few minutes. After another run, their hanging tongues indicated that they'd probably had enough and Daisy clipped on their leads and headed home.

Back at their house, she rubbed down the dogs, wiped the mud from their paws and refilled their water bowl. Then she leaned against the kitchen unit with a coffee and looked at her two charges. Her heart melted as it always did when they curled up together in their basket. She grabbed her phone and took yet another photo, grateful as ever that she loved her job so much.

Daisy always went to her parents' house for lunch on Tuesdays. She drove the twenty-five-minute journey into Kent to the rambling old building that had been her childhood home. Luckily she still had the key. No amount of ringing the doorbell could drag her mother from the studio when she was in full flow.

"Hi, Mum. Another masterpiece?"

"Hello, darling. Lay the table, will you? I'd like to get this bit finished before Mike gets back."

Daisy wasn't kidding when she said masterpiece. She knew Meirah wasn't in David Hockney's league, but she was a well established and respected artist. It sometimes made her difficult to live with, when engrossed in her projects.

By the time Daisy had laid the table, her mother had appeared, followed a few minutes later by her stepfather, Mike, who always took Tuesday afternoons off work. It was their family time together and had been ever since Daisy had decided she wanted a home of her own.

"Hello, kitten. How are things in the dog world?" asked Mike.

"Hi, Daddy. Great, and certainly better than being stuck in an office all day like you are."

"Well, somebody in this family has to have a proper job, and it definitely isn't either of you two."

He was in fact inordinately proud of them both, his wonderfully ditsy partner whom he'd been with since Daisy was just a baby, and her only slightly less ditsy daughter. As far as Mike was concerned, his ready-made family was the fulfilment of everything he'd ever wanted. As for them, he'd more than filled the vacuum left when Daisy's biological father, James, had abandoned them, and Daisy was won over from the moment Mike had swung her high above his head at their first meeting. Not only that, he was a great cook.

"So what's for lunch today? I'm famished."

"Nice of you to let me through the door before you ask. Go and talk to your mother and leave me to my kitchen. I promise you won't go hungry."

Lunch was, as ever, delicious and Daisy, wiping sauce from her chin, marvelled anew at how Mike could make even a simple spaghetti bolognese taste like something really special. It wasn't until they were at the coffee stage that her parents dropped the bombshell.

"Your father's back."

"What?"

"Your father's come back to England. He's been living in Australia, apparently." Meirah's tone was always clipped when she talked about the man who had deserted her and her child. "He wants to see you."

"As if."

"It's your decision, kitten, naturally, but it may help to lay the ghost if you meet your dad," said Mike.

"You're my dad. You've always been my dad. You didn't run off and leave us."

Daisy had no desire to meet the man who'd left his young family — for his secretary, of all people. What a cliché!

"There's a brother and sister," Mike added in as gentle a tone as he could. It made a difference. Of course it made a difference. Daisy had always yearned for siblings.

"And you knew?" she asked, horrified that they could have kept something so important from her.

"No, of course not. Your mother's heard nothing from him since he left all those years ago. He disappeared from your lives and from the country. It was news to us too."

She glanced at her mother, who remained unreadable. If meeting James meant she could meet the children she just might… Children? They'd be adults now, wouldn't they?

"I'll think about it. More coffee, anyone?"

They adjourned to the studio. Meirah liked feedback during the developmental stages of her paintings, even though the finished articles rarely bore any resemblance to the works in progress. Daisy and Mike had long ago decided that their input was of little value artistically. What did they know about colour and perspective? They just knew what they liked and didn't like, but it helped Meirah's frame of reference to discuss her work with someone else. Her latest offering was startling to say the least, but they were used to her flamboyant application of colour, although Daisy, leaning her head to one side, did say, "I wonder if you should turn it ninety degrees. I think it might look better that way."

Meirah chose to be amused rather than offended.

"I'd better go," Daisy said after another cup of coffee. "I've still got to walk Muffin. Thank God it's stopped raining."

"Bye, sweetheart." Meirah was already choosing her brush. "See you next week."

"Bye, Mum. Bye, Dad."

"You'll let us know, won't you, kitten, if you decide…" Mike trailed off. Daisy knew his only regret was that he and Meirah had never been able to give her the brother or sister she'd so desperately wanted.

"It's like I said, Dad, I'll think about it."

In reality, the decision had been made as soon as she'd heard about her siblings.

Daisy collected Muffin, a small bundle of white fur who liked almost nothing better than to roll in muddy puddles. In this weather and in spite of the protective dog coat, there was no question of a gentle rub-down when they got home. Fortunately there was a utility room with a butler sink, installed exclusively for the little dog's bath. Daisy put on a plastic coverall to protect her own clothing and she and Muffin played bubbles for a while. Putting her nose to the dog's wet black one as she lifted Muffin from the water and wrapped her in a towel, Daisy asked, "What do you think? Shall I see him? Yes or no?" The little dog moved her head far enough back to extend her tongue and give Daisy a lick that covered her face. "I take it that's a yes, then."

Daisy phoned Mike at work the next day.

"Do you think Mummy will be upset, Dad, if I meet James?"

"Truthfully, kitten, yes, I'm sure she will. I wouldn't expect her not to be, but she knows it isn't him you want to see, it's the children. There's no doubt in either of our minds that it's what you should do. You've been kept in ignorance far too long, deprived of something that's rightfully yours."

"How old are they? Do you know?"

"He didn't say."

"Come to think of it, how did he find us? I'd have thought Mummy would have dropped the phone when he rang."

"He didn't ring. At least he had that much sense. He found Mummy online. She's always painted under her maiden name. Her email address is on her website. He wrote, and I quote, *I thought you might not want to speak to me.* Astute of him, don't you think? He said he was in London, back for good maybe, and wanted to meet his little girl. HIS little girl! I'm not sure who had more steam coming out of their ears, your mother or me."

"How could he? Dad, I don't know if I can go through with this. What an abominable man."

"Well, it's possible he doesn't know about me, I suppose."

"No, it isn't. If he's looked at the website, he'd have found you there too, in her bio. If he had the sense not to phone, I'm quite sure he wouldn't have fired off an email without gathering all the information available."

"Maybe. Anyway, we're getting away from the point, which is that this isn't about him, but you have to go through him to get to your siblings. Are you ready to go ahead?"

"Yes, Daddy, I think I am."

"Shall I set it up, then? When do you want to do it?"

"I don't want to do it at all, but any day except Tuesday when I see you and Mum. Actually, Thursday's not good either. Maybe we could meet somewhere for lunch, or better still coffee — then I can just get up and leave if I want to."

"Good idea. I'll see if I can arrange it for Friday. I've got a midday appointment near home, so I won't be going back into the office. You can come running if you need to, but I'd better be there too. I don't want you and your mother throwing our best china at the walls!"

Scared as she was about the whole idea, Daisy's first thought as she ended the call was, *It's going to be a long time till Friday.*

CHAPTER TWO

Daisy was sitting drumming her fingers on the table as she waited for her father. He was twenty minutes late, and initially she'd given him the benefit of the doubt, since the trains didn't always run to schedule. But her tolerance reduced as time ticked by. Finally a man she didn't know approached her table. He looked assured, seemingly in no doubt about her identity. Daisy felt no sudden flash of recognition. She saw a well-dressed man, a little above average height, who obviously kept himself fit. She'd have passed him in the street. He meant nothing to her.

"I'm so sorry, Daisy. I got lost. I haven't had time to get my bearings yet."

James's apology was charming enough, but it had no effect on Daisy. The designated coffee shop was barely two hundred yards from the station in a straight line. Getting lost would have been difficult, and he had her number. He could have texted.

"After all these years, I don't suppose a few more minutes makes any difference. It's okay," she said, though it wasn't. She remained in her chair, terrified he would try to give her a hug, and was relieved when he sat down opposite her.

"Well. My little girl."

Daisy cringed.

"I'll just get a coffee," he said, jumping to his feet again. "Do you want another one?" he asked, looking at her empty cup.

"No, thank you. I'm fine."

Fine was the last thing she was, but no way was Daisy going to let him know that. He returned with a drink and sat down again. She studied his face, relieved that she couldn't recognise any of her own features in his. She knew she looked like Meirah, in her own opinion a watered-down version, but she didn't take account of her saucer-like hazel eyes or the pert nose that added so much to the charm of her appearance.

"You're like your mother," James said, as if reading her thoughts. So that was why he had been so sure it was her.

"Yes, I've got the out-of-control hair. I know," she said, not really wanting to have this conversation.

"It always looked good on her. How is she?"

Daisy was tempted to tell him her mother's welfare was no longer any of his business but she had another agenda and didn't want to antagonise him. "She's well, thank you. I understand you have a new family now."

"Yes, a boy and a girl. Your brother and sister."

He seemed very straightforward about it, as if he didn't want to accentuate the fact that they'd been with him all these years and she just ... hadn't. Daisy hadn't expected such consideration.

"And I believe you're thinking of remaining in England permanently."

"Yes. Well, me and Gillian, if she likes it — I don't know about Charlie and Kirsty."

Charlie and Kirsty. So now she knew their names. She ran them around in her head, like a tongue searching for the gap where a tooth used to be. Then the first part of James's sentence registered. "*If* she likes it?"

"You never know with a new place, do you? We're going to explore London and the Home Counties and see if anywhere takes her fancy."

"A new place? But I thought…"

What she thought was left unsaid, and James looked puzzled for a moment or two until the penny dropped. He had originally left Daisy and her mum for a local woman, who had them moved with him to Australia.

"Oh! Oh my goodness, no. That didn't last more than five minutes," he said. "I met Gillian in Australia soon after we arrived. Felicity came home."

Daisy was fuming. James was so offhand about the whole thing. He obviously had no idea how bad his behaviour sounded. Having left her and her mother and uprooted his secretary, he spoke as if it was perfectly okay that he'd dumped the poor woman and sent her back across the world to who knew what. There was no doubt he had a natural charm, but there was a callousness there that killed any small hope Daisy might have had of warming to the man. It was only surprising that he'd stuck with Gillian, and maybe even more surprising that she'd stuck with him. Daisy began to feel sorry for her.

"Would you like to meet Charlie and Kirsty?"

The question jolted Daisy out of her reflections, and she realised she'd been given the opening she wanted so badly. "Of course. I'd love to." *It will be interesting to meet these people who've had to put up with you for all these years*, she thought.

"I have a business appointment tomorrow morning, but I should be home by about two-thirty." Did he realise how pompous he sounded? A business appointment! "Here's the address." He scribbled it on a card. "Are you free in the afternoon? Can you make it there under your own steam?"

What a cheek! This was her city, not his. She could certainly find her way from one side of it to the other. "Yes, of course I can."

"I'll see you tomorrow then." He rose to leave and planted a perfunctory kiss on her cheek. Then he was gone, and she could only be grateful that the meeting hadn't been prolonged. She wondered why he'd bothered. He certainly didn't act like a man who wanted to renew his acquaintance with his long-lost daughter. She sat for a few minutes until she was certain that the wobble in her legs had gone and she would be able to walk.

It would be an understatement to say that Daisy was nervous. She'd been reunited with her father only yesterday after nearly twenty-nine years. Of much greater importance, though, was that she was about to meet her siblings. With a dry throat and embarrassingly shaky hands, Daisy reached up to the ornate knocker on the front door. Before she could rap it against the bronze plate, the door was wrenched open, catching her off balance. She stumbled into the arms of her host.

"Oops! Sorry. I didn't expect…"

Charlie's eyes laughed back at her. She knew it was Charlie, it had to be.

"No, it was my fault," he said. "I was looking out for you. When you didn't knock, I opened the door."

So now he knows how long I was standing on the step trying to summon up my courage, thought Daisy. *Great!*

Charlie had held Daisy's upper arms to steady her, and she felt a wave of electricity going through her body. Heat rose up her neck to her face. She tried for some composure.

"You must be Charlie. It's lovely to meet you," she said, looking up at his somewhat disarming smile. Stepping back, she held her hand out in greeting, still thinking of the feel of his strong arms about her as he'd broken her fall. "I've never had a brother before." *Or anyone for whom I had such an instant attraction. He's my brother, for goodness' sake.*

Charlie took the proffered hand. "That's a bit formal," he said, and she felt slightly foolish. "Well, I hope you're easier to get on with than my other sister."

"Don't listen to him," said a disembodied voice from behind Charlie. "I'm a pussycat really. Come in, come in. Whatever are you thinking of, Charlie, leaving Daisy standing on the doorstep? I'm Kirsty. Welcome to Wandsworth."

Daisy found herself being warmly hugged by her half-sister, a much more comfortable experience than she'd had with her brother. "Is James here?" she asked. "And your mother?"

"No, it's just us. Mum's at the hairdresser, but she'll be back soon. Dad had a meeting. He's not the greatest timekeeper."

"Yes, I found that out yesterday."

Daisy quite liked the twang of Kirsty's accent and her no-nonsense attitude. They followed Charlie into the lounge. He was sneezing. A lot.

"That's a nasty cold."

"Not a cold. Allergies. They developed during puberty, and now they won't leave me alone. Kirsty's never forgiven me, because we couldn't have another dog or even a cat." He sneezed again.

"Oh dear. I think that might be me — when you grabbed hold of me," said Daisy. This time, the red flush reached the tips of her ears. "I've probably got dog all over me."

"*All* over you?" Charlie asked.

"I walk dogs for a living. There's often a lot of romping."

"Lucky dogs."

Daisy was finding all this very disturbing. The meeting with her father the day before had been all right — there had been no spark of recognition on either side, emotionally speaking. But with Charlie things felt different.

"Dog walking! You lucky thing," said Kirsty. "I'm office-bound most of the time. What a wonderful way to earn a living."

"It's never going to make me rich, but I'd hate being cooped up all day. I started doing it as a teenager to earn a bit of pocket money and I just carried on. I didn't even go to college. I was never very good at applying myself."

"You didn't like school?"

"It wasn't that I didn't like it. But it was all so regimented, and I was a bit of a rebel."

"I don't blame you. And as for university, these days you can spend three or four years getting a degree and still not be able to get a job at the end of it."

"I'm not entirely without qualifications. I have done a course in grooming, but that was different. It involved dogs. What I'd really like is to one day work in a kennel or even own a grooming parlour. It's a bit of a pipe dream at the moment, though." How easy it was to confide in this young woman she'd only just met.

"Well, until then you're never going to be out of work. People are always going to have dogs, and working hours are getting so long that some of them never have the time to walk their pet."

"I know, and I wouldn't swap it for the world, even though I might once in a while lust after a pair of shoes I can't afford. It does have occasional disadvantages, like your brother's allergic reaction."

"Oh, but it's definitely not you I'm allergic to," Charlie put in, throwing Daisy into more confusion than ever. She was aware of her heart beating faster than normal.

He's from Australia, she thought. *It's probably just a manner of speech.*

"Could I come with you one day?" asked Kirsty.

Daisy turned her attention back to her sister, grateful for the diversion. "Of course you can. That would be lovely. Mind you, with this iffy weather you'd better make sure you're prepared for all contingencies."

"You think it's crazy here? At home, we can't anticipate what's going to happen from one hour to the next. My backpack is stuffed with clothing for all weathers, and it goes with me everywhere."

All three looked up as Gillian walked in, and Daisy's first view of her was of an immaculately dressed strong-featured woman, with blond hair swept dramatically into a chignon. She was beautiful, and just as welcoming as her children.

"Daisy, at last. I'm so sorry I wasn't here when you arrived. I was such a mess after all that travelling, and this was the first chance I've had to get to the beauty salon. James is out looking for properties and planning all sorts of excursions to the suburbs and beyond. He says it's for me, but frankly I'd rather be in town. It's my first trip to London, and I want to be in the middle of things. There'll be time enough later to move out if we want to. And you? Let me look at you... You're nothing like your father, thank goodness. Do I get a hug?"

Daisy was overwhelmed by the reception she'd received. They'd managed to exchange a lot of information, even with the four of them talking at once. Daisy and Kirsty arranged to meet on Monday for George and Mildred's walk, Kirsty having declared that Oscar was just a little early for her, as she was still suffering from jet lag. Then James arrived and Daisy couldn't believe how swiftly the atmosphere changed. One minute they were fighting to get a word in, then suddenly the exchanges became quite formal, almost cold.

"You found it okay then? Good to see you," James said to her, but there was little warmth in his greeting. Daisy was beginning to wonder why he had even bothered to contact her. Uncomfortable now, she couldn't wait to leave. Kirsty went with her to the front door.

"I can see you look puzzled," she said kindly. "I'll explain it all when I see you on Monday." She gave Daisy a quick hug before retreating into the house.

Daisy was in turmoil. It was difficult enough to adjust to her new circumstances without having to acknowledge her strange connection with Charlie — a man she couldn't have. She went straight to her parents' home. They would be anxious, she knew, to find out how she'd got on. What could she tell them? She decided to keep the bit about James to herself until after she'd seen Kirsty. She didn't want Meirah or Mike to spend the weekend worrying. In any case, her mother almost certainly wouldn't want to hear anything about the man who'd abandoned her. Instead, they all sat down to another of her father's delicious creations. Mike had prepared lamb chops with rosemary and garlic and he commented, not for the first time, that hands were invented before forks and insisted that was how they should be eaten. There was much licking of fingers as they gnawed the bones clean.

"What were they like?" Mike asked.

"Delicious as always," Daisy replied.

"Don't be obtuse. I wasn't talking about the food."

Daisy swallowed. "Oh, I think you'd like them. Mum, Gillian's very smart, with lovely blond hair that she wears in a pleat."

"And the children?" Meirah asked.

"Hardly children. I suppose Charlie must be a bit younger than me. His birthday is on twenty-ninth of February, so according to him he isn't even into double figures yet, and from the way he acts I think he's trying to prolong his childhood. Kirsty's twenty-four."

"What do they look like?"

"They're no more like James than I am. They're like their mother."

She was careful not to overdo her impression of Charlie. She thought Greek god would be probably pushing it a bit, but she'd seen the statues. Meirah was most interested in Gillian, bearing her no malice at all now that she knew she wasn't the one who had eloped with her husband.

"Will you be seeing them again soon, kitten?"

"Yes, Dad, Kirsty's meeting me on Monday. She's coming with me when I walk George and Mildred."

"And the others?"

"No, Mum, no arrangements yet, but I'm sure there will be. We all got on so well, except for James, of course. He came in later, and I left as soon as I could after he got there. He's done his bit introducing me to his family. As far as I'm concerned, I want as little to do with him as possible. My Mum and Dad are right here in this room."

There may have been a tear in Mike's eye — she couldn't be sure. It would be typical of him, a huge bear of a man with a heart of gold.

CHAPTER THREE

Over in Wandsworth, the conversation after Daisy had left was less than conciliatory.

"I've made a couple of appointments for tomorrow in Surrey, halfway between here and the coast," said James. "The car's an automatic, and I've had it insured in both our names so we can share the driving."

"You just don't listen, do you, James? I told you I wanted to stay in town but no, you have to do it your way and hope everyone will fit in with your plans," Gillian retorted. "You may as well cancel. It isn't going to happen."

"But I thought…"

"That's just the point. You didn't think. You never do. We had an agreement, and I'd be grateful if you'd stick to your side of it. And while we're at it, would it have been so hard to show just a bit more warmth towards your daughter?"

"If you two are going to have another argument, I'm out of here. Fancy a walk, Kirsty?" asked Charlie.

"Good idea," she replied. "We're not all that far from Battersea Park. I've heard it's lovely there. Hang on, I'll just get my coat. Like Daisy said, it's as well to be prepared."

They pulled on their shoes and hurried outside.

"Will those two ever sort out their problems, do you think?" said Kirsty.

"Well, frankly I think she'd be better off without him. Why she ever married him, I'll never know," Charlie replied bitterly.

"He may be my father, but unfortunately I have to agree with you. But your father hadn't long died when they met, and with you a babe in arms she must have been feeling very vulnerable."

"Yes, but why James, Kirsty?"

"I know you find it hard to believe, but he can be very charming when he wants to be."

"It's a pity he doesn't want to more often."

"No, and you couldn't describe him as a gentle man, could you? There were never any cuddles or bedtime stories when I was little, except from you and Mum."

"From what I can remember, he was hardly ever there. I guess his playing away from home didn't begin and end with Meirah. I still wonder what Mum ever saw in him."

"Come on, Charlie, we've both seen him when he's trying to impress other people, and of course he didn't tell her about Felicity when they first met. He didn't tell her anything about his past — nothing that was true, anyway. I can't imagine what a shock it must have been when she found out about Meirah and Daisy a couple of months ago."

"Enough of a shock for her to give him an ultimatum. She really wanted them to meet. Not that it seems to have done much good. He didn't seem to have any feelings for Daisy at all, did he?"

"No, and she's lovely. Maybe she's had the best of it all these years. Maybe she's the lucky one after all."

"The thing I'm most cross about, Kirsty, is that he kept her from us. All this time he had a child on the other side of the world, and we didn't even know she existed."

"Yes, I'm sure that's what upset Mum the most too. I wonder if she'll stay in England. Now you've sold the business, I rather think she fancies a complete change, from Dad as well as everything else. In my opinion, she's only stayed with him this long because of us. Now that neither of us lives at home anymore, she can finally please herself. She's certainly young and independent enough to make a new life without him and, well, I know you don't usually say this about your own mum, but she's a very attractive lady. And Dad's a good-looking man. If she does throw him out, I wouldn't be surprised if he just moves on and finds himself a rich widow."

"Poor woman — the rich widow, I mean. Look, there's the river. Isn't it beautiful?"

The next day, Daisy and Kirsty met at the park gates, as arranged. The sun came out and Daisy tied the sleeves of her anorak round her waist. Kirsty did the same. George and Mildred, delighted to have found a new game, started jumping and tugging at the dangly bits.

"I can see why you love them. It's not a bit like work, is it?"

"No, not even when the weather's awful, just as long as you're dressed for it."

They made their way to the children's play area, throwing the ball as they went.

"You said you'd explain about James," said Daisy, coming straight to the point.

"He and Mum have been having problems for a long time now. Dad's not really a people person, unless he wants something, that is."

"I'm sorry."

"Don't be. We're used to it. If I'm honest, I think we all gave up on him years ago. The thing is, he likes the ladies."

"Why does your mum put up with it?"

"Originally for our sake, I think, mine and Charlie's. After that, maybe it just became a habit."

"I'm sorry if I'm speaking out of turn, but I wondered if she couldn't afford to leave him."

Kirsty snorted. "Quite the opposite. Mum's the one with the money. Dad was useless in business, not that Charlie and I knew for years. Don't be upset, Daisy, but it was her idea to come to England, not his."

"No, I'm not. I was just surprised he was so indifferent, having supposedly travelled all this way to see me."

"Mum didn't give him a choice, not after she found out about you."

"She didn't know?"

"No, but he accidentally let the cat out of the bag. There was a photo of one of Meirah's paintings in a magazine, and he commented on how well she'd done for herself. Mum asked who she was, and he must have been wool-gathering, because he said, 'My ex-wife.' Charlie and I weren't there at the time — neither of us lives at home anymore — but I can imagine the explosion. My mum's quite an easy-going person, but she can't abide dishonesty. She'd been prepared to look away as far as his women were concerned because she'd long ago lost any love she had for him, but deception on this scale was unprecedented."

"Doesn't it upset you that he's the way he is?"

"I don't notice anymore. He's never been affectionate towards us. Once Mum knew about Meirah, it was only a short step to finding out about you. She couldn't believe he'd kept you from us. He didn't even have a photo."

"We could have visited, couldn't we?" Daisy said sadly. "We could have seen each other every few years at least. What a bastard!"

"That's exactly what Mum said. So, you see, it's Mum, me and Charlie who wanted to meet you, not Dad."

"Well, that's a huge relief, because I didn't want to see him either. Mike's my dad. I only agreed to meet James because of you. You can't imagine what it's been like, always wanting a sister and knowing you're never going to have one." Overcome by emotion, she burst into tears and Kirsty wrapped her in a huge hug, until George and Mildred began pulling at their sleeves again.

Kirsty's phone began ringing. "It's Charlie. Do you mind?"

"No, of course not."

After listening to Charlie for a couple of minutes, Kirsty said, "Daisy, Charlie wants to meet up with us. Is that okay with you?"

"Of course it is. I'd love to." Daisy felt a flutter at the thought, though.

They agreed to meet at a place by the Cutty Sark, where Greenwich met the river. Daisy took Kirsty back with her to George and Mildred's. They rubbed the dogs down, settled them in and went back to Daisy's flat so she could get changed.

"This is so cool. Have you lived here long?" Kirsty asked, looking around.

"I've been here for nearly three years now. It belongs to a friend who's studying at Yale. He didn't want to leave it empty, but he didn't want to sell it either, so he asked if I'd flat-sit for four years." She smiled, realising how strange that must sound, but Kirsty didn't seem to think so.

"Lucky you."

"Don't I know it? I pay all the bills, but it's rent-free. All I'm required to do is look after the place. In any case, it didn't seem fair to keep inflicting the extra mess on Mike, what with Mum's painting and such. She isn't the tidiest of people, and he's the one who does the clearing up."

"But it's immaculate here. Surely you didn't make a mess."

Daisy smiled. "Only when I was a teenager — who doesn't? But it was time to move out. I couldn't stay there forever."

"Were they sorry to see you go?"

"I think we all had mixed feelings. They don't live far away, and I do see quite a lot of them. They keep asking me over to eat, and Mike's a wonderful cook. Did I tell you? You don't refuse one of his invitations, but you might need to loosen your waistband afterwards."

"It all sounds lovely. We never had anything like that. Dad was always so offhand, when he was even there."

"Mum doesn't have anyone left on her side of the family, apart from me and Mike. Neither did I, until now, that is," said Daisy, smiling affectionately at her sister.

"Have you always called him Mike?"

"Never. I'm only using his name to avoid confusion. Mike's my dad, always has been."

Charlie was waiting for them when they arrived at the restaurant. They'd walked down through the park from Blackheath, had a peep at the deer enclosure, fed the ducks and took altogether far longer than they'd expected.

"I was beginning to think I'd been stood up," said Charlie. "Is everything okay?"

"It's an amazing place, Charlie. It's all my fault. I just had to keep stopping to have a look. It's just as well Daisy refused to take me up the hill to the Royal Observatory, or you might have been standing on your own for another half an hour."

"I wouldn't have minded that — there's plenty to see. I was just beginning to get a bit concerned. Who knows what might have happened?"

"You're not usually that concerned about me."

"No, but you're in a strange city. You don't know your way around."

"I had Daisy."

"Okay!" Charlie threw up his hands, admitting defeat. "I know when I'm beaten. Lunch first, or a bit of sightseeing?"

"Definitely lunch," said Daisy. "I'm starving. I always am after I've walked the dogs. Why don't we have something to eat, and then I'll show you a bit more of my home patch? Maybe I'll take you to where you can be standing on both sides of the world at the same time."

"That sounds intriguing."

"Oh, it is, Charlie, it is."

They opted for a small Italian restaurant that was a favourite of Daisy's. The food got the thumbs-up, and the accompanying wine slid down very nicely. It was a short walk from there up to the Royal Observatory and, as they stood in front of General Wolfe's statue, looking down over the river as it meandered its way through the city beneath, Daisy felt a touch of pride in her hometown. They traced picked out some of the sights that Kirsty and Charlie had previously only heard about. From there, Daisy led them to the Greenwich Meridian, where they took it in turns to stand with one foot in the western hemisphere and one in the east.

"Good heavens, is that the time?" she exclaimed after a while. "I've got to go. Muffin will be waiting for me. Can you get home all right from here? We must meet up again soon."

"We'll be fine. Are you free at all tomorrow? You make a great guide!" said Charlie.

"I always have lunch with my parents on Tuesdays." Daisy saw the expectant look on both their faces, but could hardly invite them without asking Meirah and Mike first. In any case, though her mother was pleased for her, she might not be enthusiastic about getting involved with Charlie and Kirsty. "I'll phone you later — we'll fix something up then." Daisy hurried off, glad not to have to fill a potentially awkward moment.

Reflecting that dogs had an inbuilt clock and responded well to routine, Daisy was glad she managed to get to Muffin at the usual time. She didn't want the little dog to become anxious. Muffin gave Daisy the usual wet kiss on her nose.

"You were absolutely right, Muffin," Daisy said, remembering her one-sided conversation with the dog a few days before. "James is horrible, but the rest of the family are a total delight. You may not realise it, but if it hadn't been for you I might not have had the courage to go ahead."

In the park, Muffin met some of her four-legged friends, so Daisy sat on a bench while they played. Mike would probably be home from work now. She called him.

"Hi, Dad. Good day? You both okay?"

"Your mother's trying to remove some cobalt blue paint from her left eyebrow, but otherwise everything's fine. I was just about to start preparing tomorrow's lunch. Shall I tell you what it is, or do you want it to be a surprise?"

"Surprise! Definitely!"

"How has your day been? Did the meeting with Kirsty go well?" he asked.

Daisy told him what a lovely time she'd had.

"Have you made any arrangements to see them again?"

"Charlie did ask if I was free tomorrow, but I told him I always come to you on Tuesdays."

"Well, they could come too, if you like."

She hesitated. "It's a lovely idea. I'm just wondering how Mum would feel about it."

"It should come as no surprise to you to learn that your mother and I have been discussing the situation. Of course she'd like to meet them — and I know she'd like to meet Gillian as well. That should make for an interesting conversation, don't you think? Just make sure that James doesn't come too."

"I think they'll all be pleased to go somewhere without him. As far as I can tell, they only tolerate him."

"Get on to them now then, if you can, and let me know as soon as possible. It'll need a change of plan in the kitchen, but I like a challenge."

"Are you having second thoughts? Will it be too much?"

"Are you kidding? No, it just means I'll have to pop out for a few extra things."

"I'll phone you straight back. Bye."

CHAPTER FOUR

If Meirah was the slightest bit anxious about meeting her daughter's other family, it certainly didn't show.

"Won't be long," had been her response when Daisy, having just come in, put her head round the door and reminded her mother they were expecting visitors in about ten minutes. With this Daisy had to be content, though past experience suggested the minutes would come and go unremarked. The others duly arrived, to be greeted by Daisy and Mike. He was wearing his chef's apron and waving a wooden spoon. Backing away from the door so they could enter, he gestured towards the lounge.

"It's lovely to see you all. I can't wait to have a good chat, but you'll have to excuse me for a few minutes — I'm needed in the kitchen. Daisy, take our guests in, will you, and offer them something to whet their appetites. Meirah should be with us soon, with a bit of luck."

Daisy wasn't quite so optimistic. It often took a good deal of persuasion to chisel her mother out of the studio.

"She loses track of time when she's in the middle of one of her creations," she said by way of explanation.

"I'm so envious," said Gillian. "I'd love to have some sort of artistic talent."

"We're all different, Mum," said Charlie. "You've done amazing things, like being a hugely successful businesswoman. That's a talent too."

"Why, thank you Charlie. It would have been nice, though, to write a poem or compose a song."

"And where would we have been if you had? It's not as if James would have supported us." Charlie began to sneeze.

"I suppose that's me again," said Daisy guiltily.

He pulled an inhaler from his pocket. "It might be the paint. Don't worry. This usually does the trick."

Meirah came into the room just ahead of her husband, who had discarded his apron. She was still wearing the smock that was supposed to protect what she had on underneath but rarely did. The contrast between her and Gillian couldn't have been more extreme. Meirah's unruly mop was as ever doing its own thing, whereas Gillian's hair was swept into an elegant chignon. Meirah wore a multi-coloured, loose-fitting dress beneath her smock, whereas Gillian was dressed in an immaculate mustard-coloured suit with sharp pleats in the trouser legs. What they did have in common was an overwhelming indignation that their children had been wronged and a strong desire to get on. They hit it off immediately. By the time they got to coffee, they were talking like old friends.

There was much squeaking of chairs as they were pushed back from the table.

"I did tell you that any meal of Dad's would make you need to loosen your waistband, didn't I, Kirsty?" said Daisy. "Now you know why I look like I do. The only thing that keeps it under control is the amount of exercise I get."

"Nonsense," said Charlie. "You look beautiful."

Daisy blushed at the compliment.

"I don't remember you ever saying anything like that to me," said Kirsty.

"That's because I've known you all my life and still see you as my scruffy little sister."

"Meirah, I wonder if you'd mind me throwing what's left of this Merlot at my big brother over there?"

"She wouldn't mind for a moment," said Mike before his wife could answer. "She's always splashing colours all over the place. I, on the other hand, would object most strongly. What a waste of a lovely wine. Would you like me to get the ketchup from the kitchen instead?"

Nobody wanted to leave, but as Daisy still had to walk Muffin the party broke up, though Charlie and Kirsty insisted on loading the dishwasher before they left.

"It's the least we can do, Mike, after such a wonderful afternoon. Who knows? You may even be encouraged to invite us again."

"Would next Tuesday suit you, Charlie? It's my day off. I always cook lunch on Tuesdays."

"Before you have second thoughts, yes, that would be lovely. Thank you."

"That's sounds great," said Kirsty. "I'm leaving in a few weeks, and I'd love the opportunity to get to know you better before I go."

"You're leaving, Kirsty? But I thought…" Daisy felt a shiver run through her. Had she found her family only to lose them again so soon?

"I've got a job waiting for me at home, Daisy, and a boyfriend. This was only ever going to be a holiday for me, and a chance to meet my sister. Mum and Charlie are staying, though — Charlie for a while and Mum maybe forever. Isn't that right, Mum?" she asked, looking over her shoulder.

"For a year at least, I hope. Longer if I like it and if you promise to visit."

"England will be my regular holiday destination from now on, you have my word."

"I must go. We'll talk later." Daisy rushed out of the house, trying to assimilate this unexpected and unwelcome information.

After walking Muffin, Daisy rang her friend Sam.

"Are you in this evening?" she asked. "Will Niall be there?"

"Yes, I am, and no, he won't. What's the matter, Daisy?"

"I'll tell you when I'm there. I'll just have a quick shower and then I'll be round."

An hour later, the two friends were sitting in Sam's chaotic but homely flat.

"Okay, first things first. Fancy a takeaway?"

Daisy smiled. "Dad cooked lunch today."

"That would be a no, then. Give me a minute while I prepare a magnificent feast for myself then you can spill the beans." She took a pizza from the freezer and put it in the oven. "So what's the panic? I thought everything was going well with the new family."

"It is. I can't believe how well we all get on — everyone except James. I thought now I'd found them I'd have them forever."

"But..."

"Kirsty's going back to Australia. She's only here for a holiday. She has a boyfriend to get back to, and a job. I don't want to lose her, Sam."

"Why should you lose her? You may not be able to see her very often, but a week ago you'd never even met."

"But it's so hard, finding a sister and then having to let her go. To be honest, I wouldn't care if I never saw James again, but the others are lovely. Even Gillian, who's no relation to me at all. She's as different from my mum as it's possible to be. She's tall and elegant, not a hair out of place. But you'd be amazed how well they get on. They seem to be united in their antipathy towards James, and each is indignant on the other's behalf. And apparently Charlie and Kirsty are barely talking to James."

"And they've got to live with him."

"Only while they're in England, and I'm pretty certain they'll take evasive action. Kirsty's got her own place in Australia, and I think she said Charlie does too. I'd say poor Gillian, but I rather suspect it's poor James. She's the one who holds the purse strings. Apparently my father could barely hold down a job, and Gillian is a hugely successful businesswoman. She's sold the business now and thinks she'll settle in England for a while. I kind of assumed they all would."

"So now we know where you'll be going on holiday next year. Better start saving."

"If Gillian and Charlie stay, Kirsty may come back, or maybe we could all go together."

"What does Charlie do? Doesn't he have a job to get back to?"

"I don't know, but whatever it is, there seems to be no problem with this extended visit."

"Which will give you plenty of time to get to know him better, and as for Kirsty, there's always Skype or Facetime."

"You're right. Anyway, your turn. Anything you want to talk about?"

Sam took a deep breath. "I think Niall's having an affair."

"Oh no! But he worships you."

"Not anymore, it would seem."

"And you're basing this on what? And by the way, where is he tonight?"

"On his monthly boys' night out. I'm not worried about tonight. It's the other things. He's been working late, a lot."

"So are lots of other people. It isn't easy to hold down a job these days."

"The car smelled of perfume the other day. Someone else's perfume."

"That doesn't necessarily mean anything. He could have been giving someone a lift."

"That's what he said when I asked him."

"Anything else?"

Sam teared up, and Daisy took her hand to comfort her.

"There was lipstick on his shirt collar."

"Are you telling me you never get lipstick on you? The way people air kiss these days, it's almost impossible not to. Anything else?"

"Not really. It's just everything put together."

"It isn't like you to get so worked up, Sam. Normally it would take a rhinoceros to knock you off your stride. Are you pre-menstrual?"

Sam blushed.

"Sam? SAM! Are you *pregnant?*"

"Niall doesn't know. And you're not to tell him."

"But that's wonderful news!"

"Or not. What if he doesn't love me anymore? What if he wants to split up? He's not to know until I'm sure. I'm not having him stay with me for the sake of a baby. If I have to, I'll manage on my own. Your mum did, after James left. Well, until Mike came along, anyway."

"I think you're mad. You've blown this out of proportion. How can you not tell Niall? He'll be thrilled."

"Not until I'm sure, Daisy. Promise me."

"Of course, if that's what you want. In the meantime, I'm here if you need me."

CHAPTER FIVE

"What happened to talk later?" Charlie demanded when Daisy answered his call the next day. "Your phone kept diverting to voicemail."

"Why didn't you leave a message, Charlie?"

"Because that would have given you the chance to think up an excuse, and I didn't want you to say no. Fancy a ride on an open-topped bus?"

"Are you *mad*?"

"Probably. But the sun's come out, and they do those wonderful running commentaries on the hop on, hop off thing."

"Then you don't need me as a guide."

"Of course I do, for the hopping off." He had an answer for everything. "Kirsty's going Oxford Street, shopping with Mum. I need you, Daisy."

"Then how can I refuse? But I won't be free until one. Shall we meet at Charing Cross? It's easy enough for both of us. We'll have the whole of the rest of the day, if you're free."

"For you, always."

Now why did he have to say that?

Daisy had a lot of time to think during her three morning walks. She was looking forward to the rest of the day with somewhat mixed feelings. She'd admitted to herself that her pleasure in Charlie's company was more than that of a sister for a brother. How awful was that? Charlie had appeared in her life just weeks after the failure of her last dismal relationship, and now she was filled with despair. The fact that he was her brother was an insurmountable problem. She'd probably be able to cope better if only he wasn't so nice to her, almost as if he was feeling it too, but he *was* Australian. She was sure they didn't suffer from the same inhibitions as the English. He was probably this nice to every young woman he met.

Charlie also had lots of time to think. When he remembered how close the National Gallery was to Charing Cross, he decided to pay another visit while he waited, having barely scratched the surface when he'd been with Kirsty. Gazing at so many masterpieces filled him with admiration, but a vision of Daisy kept creeping to the front of his mind. Every time he was in the same room as her, the air seemed to fill with joy. The fact that he also suffered a sneezing fit every time they met seemed not to matter.

Looking at his watch, Charlie realised he was going to be late if he didn't hurry, and he bolted through Trafalgar Square, almost getting himself run over as he raced across The Strand and into the station in time to see Daisy coming through the ticket barrier. She saw him immediately.

"I think the bus stops just opposite the station, unless you want to go to Trafalgar Square first or maybe walk down The Mall to Buckingham Palace," she said when she'd reached him.

"The Palace sounds good. I had a flying visit around the National Gallery while I was waiting for you. A whole day wouldn't be enough to get round there, though, would it? Maybe we can go together another time."

"Yes, I haven't been for ages. I love the Tate Britain as well."

By this time they'd gone through Admiralty Arch into The Mall, and the tarmac drew them like a red carpet towards the official royal residence. "It feels a bit like the yellow brick road, only red," said Charlie. "I wonder what will happen if I click my heels together, like Dorothy in *The Wizard of Oz*?"

"A sprained ankle, probably."

"Where's your sense of adventure?"

"Just because I don't have a fancy to meet any wicked witches. Oh, right. I've just realised. You want to get back to Oz."

"Actually no, Daisy. Since we sold the business for an indecent amount of money, my time is pretty much my own, for a while at least. You did know I was a partner, didn't you? I'd like to do something else eventually, but for the time being I'm taken by the spirit of adventure. I want to see the world. Mum and I worked all hours to make the company a success. It's good to be able to reap the benefits."

"I didn't realise you were that wealthy."

"We've done pretty well for ourselves. It's funny, isn't it? If James hadn't been like he was, Mum would never have discovered her talent for commerce and achieved so much. It's a property company, nationally known, and she built it up from nothing. I'm so proud of her."

"I can see why you would be. And you're probably underestimating your own contribution."

"It's always been said that money makes money. The company was pretty much established by the time I joined, but yes, I've done my bit too. Oh my goodness, will you look at that!" He stared up at Buckingham Palace. "Wow! Is all that gold for real?" Charlie was looking at the intricate wrought iron surrounding the building, lavishly decorated with gold leaf.

"It is a bit ostentatious, isn't it?" said Daisy.

"It's amazing. We don't have anything like this back home. Can we go inside?"

"There are a couple of months in the year, during the summer when the royal family isn't in residence, when they run tours — not of the private apartments, of course. If it's opulence you like, it'll really suit you. I went a few of years ago."

"Will you come with me if I'm still here?"

"Of course I will. But that's four months away. I expect you'll be long gone by then."

"Not gone, as such. Possibly travelling. There are so many places in Europe I want to see. It'd be nice to have company. Do you fancy the Grand Tour?"

"I think Oscar and the rest might have some objection to that."

"Oscar?"

"One of the dogs I walk."

"Oh, for the minute I thought there was a man in your life."

"There was, until quite recently. It didn't work out. So you can imagine how grateful I am to have a brother to look after me."

Unaware that Daisy thought they were blood relatives, disappointment kicked Charlie in the gut. *Well, if it's a brother she wants, a brother I'll have to be*, he thought. He'd been hoping that she felt their connection too. He still remembered the delightful flush on her cheeks the first time they'd met, the tingle that had passed between them when he'd grabbed hold to steady her. He'd read too much into it, obviously. Perhaps it was just her British reticence that had caused her colour to rise.

"Do you want me to sort him out for you? Is he bigger than me?"

Daisy laughed. "No, I do not, thank you very much. It was just … well, I thought at the time…" Her voice petered out as she remembered Jonathan. He had been solid and safe, always attentive — opening doors, holding out her chair, helping her on with her coat. There'd been no excitement, though. Finally, she'd summoned the courage to admit to herself that this wasn't what she wanted out of life. It had been harder summoning up the courage to tell Jonathan.

Charlie's voice broke in on her thoughts. "Daisy, I'm really hungry. Is there somewhere we could go to eat?"

"Let's head for Leicester Square," she suggested. "It's not too far, and there are plenty of restaurants. Afterwards, maybe Shaftesbury Avenue."

"I hope you're not forgetting my bus ride. It isn't that I don't want to walk, but there's something magical about seeing a city from the top of a bus, and having someone telling you through crappy headphones a little bit about each place."

"You're just a big kid, aren't you?" she said, laughing. Charlie's excitement was infectious. "Okay, after lunch the bus it shall be."

At ten o'clock, they were back on the concourse at Charing Cross Station.

"Are you sure you don't want me to take you home?" asked Charlie.

"Yes, I'm sure, thank you very much. It's no distance to walk from the station at the other end, and it makes no sense for you to come to Blackheath. You'd have to come all the way into town again, I think, to get back to Wandsworth."

"Text me when you get in then, just so I know you're okay."

Daisy was touched by this concern for her safety as he leaned forward and kissed her on the cheek. "It's been a wonderful day, Charlie. Thank you."

"I don't suppose you could alter the time of Muffin's walk so we can do this again? I'm sure Mum and Kirsty would love to see London like this."

"I could ask, I suppose. It might actually make more sense, breaking up the day for her, though I usually feed her as well."

Daisy was running through the options in her mind as she spoke. "I'll ask, and yes, I'll text you later. Night."

It took Daisy a while when she woke the next morning to realise why she was feeling so good. The sunlight was streaming in through the gap in the curtains. Spring was on its way at last, and there was definitely a spring in Daisy's step as she bounced into the bathroom to brush her teeth. She glanced at herself in the mirror. *Look at me, foaming at the mouth. I might as well be*, she thought. *It's madness spending time in Charlie's company when I'm only going to be hurt. Bugger it, I don't care. I'm going to make the most of every moment. In a few months, he'll be gone. I'll worry about it then.* And with surprising cheerfulness, Daisy tripped off down the road to collect Oscar.

Daisy was sitting on a bench and enjoying the sunshine with Oscar when her phone beeped. She looked at the message. It was from Charlie: *Mum and Kirsty would love to come out with you.*

No chance to talk about Muffin yet, she texted back. *Can do 2-4 on Thursday.*

You're on, he replied.

Daisy had never been on the London Eye herself, so the experience was as good for her as it was for her family, once Kirsty had summoned the courage to move from the middle to the edge of the pod.

"Just don't look down and you'll be fine," Daisy said, trying hard not to pull her hand out of Kirsty's vice-like grip. And she was fine. The view was spectacular, made all the more enjoyable for Daisy by Charlie standing behind both women with a comforting arm around each.

Back on the ground, she gave them all a quick hug and rushed off, promising to contact them later.

"Sorry, I really can't stop. The queuing took longer than I thought it would. If I were you, I'd walk that way," she said, pointing in the direction of the Southbank Centre. "The atmosphere's amazing, and there are loads of things to see. You might want to check what's on at The National Theatre. We could go tomorrow, maybe?"

Daisy waited until seven o'clock before phoning Muffin's owner, Eunice.

"I was wondering if we might change our arrangements a bit."

"You're not leaving us, are you? Muffin adores you." Daisy could hear the alarm in her voice.

"And I adore her too. No, Eunice, it's just that I wondered if she might benefit from me coming earlier so that she's not on her own for quite so long."

"It sounds like a good idea. Won't it be bad for her to wait for her feed, though, until we get home from work?"

"Well, I've been thinking, as she's such a little soul, it might be better to split her feeds three ways. Then it wouldn't be too late at all."

"It sounds okay to me. You know Muffin comes first in this house."

Daisy did, remembering the specially installed bathroom for the little dog. "Okay, shall we try it tomorrow? See how it works? The only thing you need to do is divide her food differently. I'm sure it'll be best for her."

As she finished her call, her mobile rang again.

"Daisy, it's Sam. Can you talk?

"Of course I can. Do you want me to come over?"

"Oh, could you?"

Daisy hurried out and once again found herself sitting in her friend's lounge.

"Have you told Niall yet?" she asked.

"No, of course not. I said I wouldn't before, and it's worse now."

"In what way?"

"He's going away for a few days. To Birmingham."

"Sam, he's always gone to Birmingham. His company has offices there. He's been doing that ever since he started working for them."

"But I didn't know there was anything wrong before."

"You don't know there's anything wrong now. Sam, you have to get a grip. You'll make yourself ill with all this worry. It won't do you or your baby any good."

"He's going for an extra day this time."

"So what? It just means there's more to do. Give the guy a break. He's been with you for seven years."

"And we've all heard of the seven-year itch."

"Has anyone at your office noticed anything different about you?"

"No. Somebody said I looked a bit peaky, but there's a lot going around, so I don't think anyone suspects anything yet."

"And your parents? What do they think about the prospect of their first grandchild?"

"They don't know yet," Sam said guiltily. "The moment after they know, Niall will know, which brings me back to square one."

"So it's just me."

"Yes, Daisy, just you."

"Then I'd better do something about getting to the bottom of this, hadn't I? Why don't you invite me, Charlie and Kirsty over for a meal on the pretext of wanting to meet them? I'm sure they'd love to come."

"And what do I do when Niall asks why I'm not drinking?"

"Just have one glass and pretend. I'm sure a tiny drop on your lips won't do the baby any harm."

"What about Sunday lunch, then? I never drink in the middle of the day, so he definitely won't make anything of it."

"Great. When's he going away?"

"Sunday night, as it happens."

"Excellent. If there are any signs of a guilty conscience, I'll be sure to notice. Shall I see if they can come then?"

"Yes, please. Call them now. Invite Gillian too."

Daisy phoned Kirsty and received an enthusiastic response.

"They'd love to," she told Sam when she'd ended the call. "And apparently tomorrow we're going to the National Theatre. Now, do you need any help with this lunch? Can I bring something over?"

"Not unless you can persuade your dad to cook. Now, there's an idea. Why don't they come too, your mum and dad? I haven't seen them for ages."

"Don't you think it'll be a bit too much for you?"

"Not a bit. If Mike's coming, he won't be able to stop himself bringing one of his specials. I could do nothing and there'd still be enough to feed a small army."

"That's true. Go on then. You phone them. It's been a busy two days. I'm going home to curl up with a book before I go to sleep," Daisy said, picking up her coat and dropping a kiss on the top of her friend's head. She'd had every intention of confiding her feelings about Charlie, but Sam had enough problems at the moment. And in any case, there was nothing she could do.

CHAPTER SIX

On Friday, Daisy received a call from Gillian.

"I'm so looking forward to the theatre this evening, but I didn't want to leave it until then to speak to you," she said.

"Anything wrong?"

"No, but it's Saturday tomorrow. The car's just sitting outside in the bay, so we're thinking of going for a drive in the country. We wondered if you could come with. You don't dog walk at the weekends, do you?"

"No, I don't, but you'll be getting fed up with me at this rate."

"Are you trying to tell me something?"

"Am I…? Good grief, no. I'm having a lovely time getting to know you all."

"Well, it cuts both ways. We've travelled thousands of miles to see you and we want to make the most of every minute. Any suggestions as to where we should go?"

"There are several beautiful places in Surrey. I could get a train to Wandsworth and we can go from there."

"Why don't you bring an overnight bag this evening? We've got plenty of room here."

"I'm not sure."

"Because of James?"

"Frankly, the less I see of him the better I'll like it."

"He's gone to stay with some old friends for a few days. At least, that's what he said, but I think he's just keeping out of our way. He's behaving like a spoilt child since I managed to convince him I had no intention of living in the country. If I told him where we were going for the day, he'd think I was being perverse."

"Look, I know it's none of my business…"

"Since there's no love lost between the two of you, I can tell you that I can't believe he's hung on for as long as he has. I wish he'd leave me. In the end I may have to initiate a legal separation. There's one good thing, though: if he'd gone earlier, I'd never have found a wonderful new daughter I didn't even know existed. Pack that bag, Daisy. I'll see you later."

As they sat eating toast and marmalade in the big kitchen in Wandsworth on Saturday morning, Daisy was hard put to believe it was only a week ago she'd met them all for the first time.

"I absolutely loved the play last night," said Gillian. "I'm so glad we didn't pick a tragedy."

"You're right, Mum," said Charlie. "We all know some of Shakespeare's plays are really hard going, but *A Midsummer Night's Dream* is great fun, and the National Theatre is amazing. Mind you, I'd love to see something at the Globe."

"I don't think I'd want to be one of the seven-hundred people standing all the way through, though." Gillian looked at her watch. "Has everyone finished eating? We'll go in ten minutes, then."

There was plenty of room in the back of the large car but, even though there were two feet between her and Charlie, Daisy imagined she could feel the electricity between them. The feeling stayed with her all day as they took in the beautiful landscaped gardens of Surrey.

"We don't have anything like this at home. Are there many more we could see?" Charlie asked her.

"The country's littered with them, though sadly some have fallen into disrepair. We could visit one a week from March, when most of them open, to the beginning of November and still not get through them all."

"What a shame Kirsty's going back soon. Look how she and Mum are enjoying themselves."

Brought up short by the reminder, Daisy halted her stride and Charlie was several feet ahead of her before he realised she wasn't beside him anymore.

"What's wrong? Did I say something wrong?"

"I can't get my head round the fact that she's leaving. I suppose you think I'm being very selfish."

"Not selfish at all. If I thought you were going somewhere, I'd be the same. I'm afraid you'll just have to rely on me instead. I can't imagine her being so far away — we've always been so close. And now there's you, Daisy. Maybe we could Skype her every week, you and me. That way we'd at least feel as if we're all together."

Daisy tried to lighten things up. "Ah, but Kirsty came and walked the dogs with me. It's not like you're going to do that, is it?"

"I'll wear a mask. Will that do?"

She laughed. "That should be a pretty sight."

"I mean it, Daisy. Look, I've been sneezing enough today, haven't I? It doesn't take very much to set me off, but I don't let it rule my life. If I want to walk with you, I will. If it's okay with you, that is."

On Sunday, Daisy breathed in deeply as Sam opened the door to her, Gillian and her siblings. "Something smells wonderful," she said.

"Now, there's a compliment. Meirah and Mike aren't here yet, so it must be mine. Come on in, everyone. It's lovely to meet you all. Niall's just finishing packing. He'll be with us in a minute."

"You're going away?" asked Charlie. "Somewhere nice?"

"No, he's off on business for a few days. His job sends him all over the country."

No-one other than Daisy would have noticed the slight undertone.

"That must be tedious. I used to be the same. Couldn't wait to get back home again."

Daisy was introducing the rest of her family when Niall appeared and the doorbell rang. He did an about-turn and opened the door to Meirah and Mike.

"It's great to see you again," he said as he embraced Meirah. "It's been far too long."

"Get off with you, you and your Irish blarney," she said, but he was an old favourite and she hugged him back. He shook hands with Mike and then with the rest of the guests as introductions were resumed. Daisy got a big hug like her mother had.

"Put me down, you great oaf. I'm suffocating here."

"Mike, haven't you forgotten something?"

"Forgotten what, Meirah? Good grief, yes! Excuse me, I've left my contribution in the car." He was back in no time, carrying a huge dish. "Daisy said it would be all right if I brought something."

"All right, Mike? I've been relying on you!"

Niall offered round drinks and pretty soon they'd moved to the table. Mike's dish took pride of place in the centre of Sam's buffet.

Niall had his back to the room, the last to serve himself at the buffet, and Sam raised an eyebrow at Daisy. She shook her head ever so slightly, but the gesture was picked up by Charlie, who found himself wondering what it was all about. He was sitting across the table from Daisy, and as she turned to talk to her mother, Charlie took pleasure in admiring her profile. Four hours and a lot of surreptitious glances later, the visitors reluctantly took their leave, aware that Niall had a train to catch.

"Can we give you a lift to the station, Niall?" Gillian offered.

"Thank you, Gillian, but I'm just going to have a quiet coffee with Sam before I go. I won't be back until Wednesday, and I miss her when I'm away. It's been great meeting you all, though. We must do it again soon. I can't remember the last time I enjoyed myself so much, or ate so much! I'm only sorry we've had to cut it a bit short."

"Well, I'll do the honours next time, as long as I can rely on Mike to make another contribution," said Gillian warmly. "Have a good trip. It's been lovely."

Once outside, they all decided to adjourn to Meirah and Mike's. It was out of the way, but everyone was in such good spirits that it seemed a shame to break up the party. This time, they had an opportunity to see more of Meirah's work. There were canvases everywhere in her studio, one alcove holding more than twenty, which were lined up like books on a shelf.

"May I?" Charlie asked.

"Of course."

He looked at them all, occasionally pulling one out and holding it up for scrutiny. "They're amazing, Meirah."

"Help yourself if there's one you particularly like. As you can see, I'm a bit overrun."

"I couldn't possibly," he said, but his fingers riffled through until he came to one he'd obviously had his eye on. "Unless … I don't suppose … is this one too personal?"

He'd chosen a portrait of Daisy as a child of about five, instantly recognisable in spite of Meirah's somewhat flamboyant style and artistic licence.

"She's always been my favourite subject. You can't imagine how many I have of her. Of course, take it. I'd be delighted."

"Well, I'm not sure I would be delighted, scruffy little toad that I was," Daisy protested.

"You keep out of this. It's between me and your mother."

Secretly Daisy was very touched, but Charlie wasn't sure how to proceed.

"Can I… Will you accept… I'd like to…"

"Don't talk such rubbish. Just make sure you give it a nice frame and, if you must, make a donation to charity. Let that be an end to it."

"Thank you. I will."

Daisy's phone rang. It was Sam. She excused herself and left the room.

"What do you think, Daisy? Am I right?"

"Right off your trolley. He's as loving and attentive as always."

"That's what I'm worried about. He's a bit too loving and attentive. What did you think about him saying he misses me when he's away?"

"I think it's exactly what he meant. You're reminding me of those awful drama classes at school. Stop looking for trouble where there isn't any."

Sam burst into tears, and Daisy was filled with remorse.

"I'm so sorry, Sam. I didn't mean to upset you, but I really think you're making a mistake here. Your hormones are all over the place because you're pregnant. Look, why don't I come over and stay with you tonight? I'm sure Gillian will drop me off when they go."

"They're still with you?"

"Yes, we came back to Mum's to look at her paintings. I'll get a lift home, pick up a toothbrush and walk round."

"If you're sure."

"What are friends for? You'd do the same for me."

They were sitting at either end of Sam's sofa, both cross-legged. Sam wasn't crying anymore, but she was definitely subdued.

"You won't be able to do that for much longer."

"Do what?"

"Sit like that, with your legs crossed. A little somebody in there is going to start protesting."

A smile chased away the gloom on Sam's face. "I am so excited, Daisy. It's the biggest thing that's ever happened to me, apart from Niall."

"And he should be sharing this with you, Sam. You have to tell him." Daisy hadn't wanted to upset her friend again, but it had to be said. She watched the smile flee as quickly as it had come.

"Not until I'm sure. Tell me the truth, Daisy. What did you think?"

"Exactly what I told you on the phone. The man's besotted. In any case, the Niall I know couldn't tell a lie to save his life. Why are you so worried all of a sudden?"

"I can't really put my finger on it. It's a lot of little things, little attentions that weren't there before."

"You don't know how lucky you are. I wish I had someone who would shower little attentions on me like that."

"But you did. You had Jonathan."

Daisy snorted and Sam giggled. Jonathan had never had Niall's spontaneity.

"How far along are you?"

"Ten weeks."

"And you're worried that Niall is being so nice to you because he has a bimbo hidden away somewhere?"

"I'm thinking that he has someone like us. I can't really see Niall with a bimbo."

"And nor can I. How would he be able to juggle two relationships when he's so committed to this one? You're not thinking straight — you're pregnant, for goodness' sake. Tell him, Sam."

"I don't want to blackmail him into staying for the baby's sake, Daisy. I couldn't bear it."

There was no consoling her friend that night, so they watched a girly film to take their minds off the problem and went to bed. Sam slept like a log. Daisy lay awake for most of the night. She didn't for one second believe Niall was having an affair, or even thinking about it. What did worry her was that when he found out about his impending fatherhood, Sam would convince herself she'd been right. There seemed to be no way round it at the moment.

CHAPTER SEVEN

When the family met up the following afternoon, Kirsty presented Daisy with a ball-thrower.

Daisy was delighted. "Brilliant! That's so nice of you. I insist you get up early tomorrow and come and meet Oscar, the true recipient. He's like a big teddy bear."

"We'd love to," said Charlie, though the invitation had been directed at his sister.

"What about your allergies?"

He just took his inhaler out of his pocket and waved it at her.

"Fair enough. Eight o'clock at mine."

The next morning, Oscar accepted his enlarged escort as no more than his due, greeting each newcomer in turn. Charlie was enchanted.

"He's great. I'll just have to get something stronger prescribed so I can do this more often."

"Are you telling me that for all these years I've gone without a dog when you could have done something about it?" Kirsty demanded.

"Great strides have been made in allergy medication since I was a boy, Kirsty," he teased.

Charlie and Daisy stood outside the coffee shop while Gillian and Kirsty went in for hot drinks and muffins. Oscar strained at the lead in frustration until Charlie told him to sit in a very firm voice. Oscar recognised authority when he heard it. He obeyed, to Daisy's amazement.

When Gillian and Kirsty returned, the four of them found two benches close together in the park, and the dog was let off his lead while they had their picnic. Once he'd run around for a few minutes, he returned to sit in front of Charlie, with one paw on his knee.

"I think he's trying to tell me something," said Charlie. "Have you got that ball launcher handy, Daisy?"

She passed it to him, and he went off to play with the dog while the three women gathered on one bench to talk.

An hour later, they left Daisy at Oscar's door. She needed to walk George, Mildred and Muffin, and the others wanted to find a suitable gift to take with them to Meirah and Mike as a thank-you for the anticipated lunch. Daisy met them in the village when she had completed her walks, and they made their way to her parents' house.

The party finally broke up at eleven o'clock that night, after an extended lunch and a late supper.

Gillian groaned as she lowered herself into the driving seat of the hire car. "I've never eaten so much or been so unfit. Any chance you can you recommend a gym, Daisy?"

"Not in Wandsworth. I don't know the area very well at all."

"Are you two going to join me?" Gillian asked her children, who were being uncharacteristically quiet.

"I'm going to get my exercise dog-walking with Daisy, if she'll have me," Charlie replied, whereas Kirsty quite rightly said that it wasn't worth her taking out membership as she was going home soon.

"It's just me for the treadmill, then," said Gillian as she pulled up outside Daisy's home. "Are you free at all tomorrow, sweetheart?"

"I really need to do some catching up," Daisy replied, to the disappointment of them all, herself included. "Although I could rustle something up in the evening, if you'd like to come.

It won't be up to Dad's standard, but most of us lesser mortals don't aspire to those heights."

It was agreed. Daisy was delighted. Even if she wasn't in her dad's class, she was a good cook.

Daisy slept well and woke ready to take on the world. She liked entertaining and was looking forward to her afternoon trip to the supermarket. Five minutes before she was due to leave to collect Oscar, the bell rang and she opened the door to find Charlie standing outside.

"What on earth are you doing here?"

"That's not quite the reception I was hoping for. We had an arrangement, didn't we?"

"Arrangement?"

"Sure. Mum would go to the gym, and I would come with you to walk the dogs."

"You were serious!"

"Of course I was. In any case, I've completely lost my heart to Oscar. Come on then. We don't want to keep him waiting, do we?"

"Okay, but I'm not sharing my wages with you."

"The pleasure of your company will be payment enough for me."

"Nonsense. You're just a big kid. Your payment will be playing with Oscar."

It was all she could think of to turn aside his compliment, one of a growing number that she was finding it increasingly hard to cope with. Fortunately, he was overtaken by a bout of sneezing, which took any awkwardness out of the situation.

"You obviously haven't been to the chemist yet. I'll see if I can pick something up from the supermarket when I go shopping this afternoon."

As they set off down the road, Charlie said he was hoping to spend the day with her. "My mother and my sister have deserted me, so I'm a lost soul at a loose end in a foreign country. You may be the only member of my family I can rely on."

Daisy felt far more comfortable with this sort of clowning and readily accepted his company. Now that she was on even keel again, the hours fled by. That evening, he acted as her sous-chef, and by the time Gillian and Kirsty arrived they were on their second glass of wine and very much at ease in each other's company.

"Help your poor mother to a chair, Charlie. I can hardly walk," Gillian said, but the smile in her eyes belied her words. "*And* the people at the gym suggested I go three times a week. If it doesn't kill me, I shall expect to be at least fit enough to take part in the next marathon."

"I notice you haven't mentioned that I suffered with you," said Kirsty. "When I told them I didn't want to take out membership, they told me I could go in with a visitor's pass. So instead of sitting down to wait with a cup of coffee, I found myself being dragged into the gym as well. Ah, wine. That'll help."

Charlie put a glass into her hand.

Partway through the evening, Daisy got a text from Sam: *Niall's home. He's being soooo solicitous. I'm scared.*

Daisy replied: *House full of visitors. I'm sure it's okay. I'll call you tomorrow.* She hoped her friend would be all right until then.

Daisy received another text from Sam early the next morning: *Can you meet me for lunch? The pub next to my office. 1pm.*

Charlie's walking the dogs with me. Think he plans to stay, Daisy replied.

Bring him with, Sam wrote.

With this Daisy had to be content, though there was nothing in Sam's messages to indicate whether there was good news or bad.

"You seem a bit distracted this morning. Is anything wrong?" asked Charlie.

"Nothing at all. I think this balmy spring sunshine is making me sleepy."

"Not last night's copious quantities of alcohol then?"

"Definitely not that." She smiled up at him, her heart somersaulting. The only downside of the evening had been Kirsty's comment that she must book her ticket home, not for next week but definitely the one after. Apart from anything else, she was missing her boyfriend, Cam.

"What am I going to do without Kirsty? In no time she's become such a big part of my life that I can't imagine her not being here."

"Don't worry," said Charlie. "I'll be hounding you so much that you'll wish you'd never met any of us."

"No, I'd never wish that. Your mother's lovely." They both laughed, then Daisy told him about Sam's invitation to lunch.

"Are you sure it isn't private? She seemed to have something on her mind when we were there on Sunday."

Obviously not much got past him.

"It's fine. She's expecting you. I accepted on your behalf — sorry if I did the wrong thing."

"No, I'd love to see her again. Is Niall back yet?"

"Yes. He came back last night."

"Perhaps we could go out for a meal with them, just the four of us, after Kirsty's gone back?"

"I'm sure they'd like that," she said, wishing she could be sure of anything, mostly that her friends would still be together.

The rest of the morning passed in a whirl of dog-walking, ball-throwing and rubbing down, or in Muffin's case bathing. Charlie was gifted the obligatory lick on the nose, which he took in good part, though it did provoke another bout of sneezing. For the most part the new tablets were working well, but this was extreme provocation.

Sam was waiting when they arrived at the pub for lunch.

"I was hoping you wouldn't be late. I'm starving, but I didn't want to start without you."

Daisy was reassured. Her friend seemed to be in good spirits. Her large appetite was something new, no doubt due to her pregnancy. They studied the menu and Charlie went to the bar to order. Sam seized the opportunity to talk to her privately.

"It's all okay, Daisy. I was wrong."

"Tell me something I don't know."

Sam giggled. "He's known all the time. He found the pregnancy test in the bin. It never occurred to me to wrap it up or throw it where he wouldn't see. His extra attentions have been because of the baby."

"That's fantastic. What made you decide to tell him after all?"

"I didn't. He was so worried while he was in Birmingham that he just blurted it out when he got back. He couldn't understand why I hadn't told him. He was really upset, but when I explained he just burst out laughing. I've been such a fool. Oh, Daisy, I'm so happy!"

"As you deserve to be."

Charlie came back armed with drinks and said lunch wouldn't be long.

"Sam has something to tell you, Charlie."

"I'm pregnant," she said, glowing with pride.

"That's wonderful news. It suits you."

And it did. Now that her fears were gone, Sam was positively radiant.

"Niall and I talked about it last night. We're going round to my parents later to tell them, but I wanted Daisy to know everything was okay."

Charlie raised his glass. "I think a toast is called for. To Sam and Niall, their baby and their future."

CHAPTER EIGHT

The following Sunday, Gillian fulfilled her promise to host lunch and Mike kept his by bringing two huge dishes. Daisy had accepted a lift with Sam and Niall, as they were nearer than her parents. The success of the previous week was repeated, until midway through the afternoon when everyone was shocked to see James walk in. As one they rushed to fill the awful silence their surprise had induced. James seemed unperturbed and in his most affable manner welcomed everyone to his home. Meirah was the only one who hadn't spoken. The colour had drained from her cheeks, and had it not been for Mike, who flung his arm around her shoulder, Daisy thought she would have got up and left.

"It's lovely to see you again, Meirah. You haven't changed a bit. And you must be Mike. Nice to meet you."

What little sense James had stopped him from offering his hand. Just as well, since Mike would probably have twisted it behind its owner's back and pulled hard. As it was, he didn't even bother to acknowledge the greeting.

"And Daisy. From what I hear, you've got to know the rest of the family now. I'm so glad it's all worked so well."

Not many things rendered Daisy speechless, but that certainly did. Gillian stepped into the gap.

"James, I wonder if you'd mind helping me with something in the kitchen."

You could have heard a pin drop in the dining room. No-one wanted to be the first to speak. Sam and Niall had never met James, of course, and this charming man seemed to be nothing like their friend's description of him. Meirah was looking like a rabbit caught in a car's headlights and her daughter rushed round the table to comfort her.

"How could he do this to you, Mummy? It's unforgivable. Daddy, I don't know how you didn't punch him on the nose."

"It was a close thing, I can tell you, but I am a guest in his house and I wouldn't demean myself. The truth is, I think it would have upset your mother even more."

The arm he'd held round her shoulder was now comforting rather than restraining.

"The worst is over now, Meirah. He can't hurt you anymore. I'm sure Gillian will deal with him. Here, why don't you have a sip of brandy?" he said, looking up at Charlie, who provided the restorative immediately.

"Anyone else?" Charlie asked and, Sam being the only exception, they all willingly fortified themselves. "After all, you're supposed to have liqueurs after a meal, aren't you?"

It took some time and effort by the stronger members of the group to bring the others back to a semblance of reality. Between them Charlie, Niall and Mike restored the balance, and though they were all aware that James was in the next room, they did their best to act normally.

After ten minutes, Gillian returned to her visitors. "I'm so sorry," she said. "You won't be bothered by him again. He's leaving, and he won't be coming back."

Kirsty moved to comfort her mother, who was shaking.

Daisy was astonished to find a text message from James on her mobile when she got home. It said, *Please call. Urgent.* Angry though she was, Daisy didn't have it in her to ignore the word urgent. Her anger became full-blown rage when James told her what he wanted.

"I can't believe you're asking me such a thing."

"I don't have anywhere else to go, Daisy."

"It's out of the question. Haven't you done enough damage already? Find a hotel, or one of those old friends you keep visiting. Goodnight!"

Daisy grabbed her coat on the way to answer the doorbell the next morning, expecting to see Charlie waiting to go on their by now almost daily walks. Instead, she found James. He looked awful, unshaven and unkempt.

"What the hell are you doing here?" she demanded. "Didn't I tell you not to come?"

"I slept on a park bench. It was freezing. I can't go back to the house without checking with Gillian first and she's not answering my calls."

"And who can blame her? Okay, come in. I can't supply a razor, but you can go and have a wash and I'll make you some breakfast. There's an unopened toothbrush in the bathroom cabinet. That's it, though. After that, you're out. And be quick, I have to go to work."

James had just sat down at the table when the bell rang again. Charlie's smile turned to fury when he saw James, then to bewilderment as he looked to Daisy for an explanation. What explanation could there possibly be? He turned and left. Daisy was crushed. There were few things she could have said to Charlie, none of which would have been acceptable. She didn't have the heart to throw James back out onto the street, but she should have done. She knew what sort of a man he was, and now, even if Charlie didn't think she was siding with her father, the evidence at least indicated that she was supporting him.

"I'm surprised to see him here so early in the morning," James said, totally oblivious to anyone's needs but his own.

"That's it! I want you to leave now."

"But I haven't finished my breakfast."

"You know what, I'm glad I didn't have to live with you all these years. You're impossible. Out! Now! And please don't contact me again."

A short while later, Daisy was stumbling along the street with Oscar, blinded by her tears. *Charlie thinks I'm helping James*, she thought. *He'll tell the others and they'll think so too. He must hate me. They'll all hate me.*

Oscar looked behind Daisy for Charlie.

"Sorry, but he isn't here. He probably won't ever be here again."

Her renewed bout of crying earned her some sympathy from the dog. It wasn't until they were in the park that she'd composed herself enough to try and think. She fired off a text to Charlie: *Please phone. It isn't what it looked like.* His reply came back immediately: *I just can't at the moment. I need time to think.*

It was possibly the bleakest day of Daisy's life. She kept checking her phone in case she'd missed a call or a text. Everyone was supposed to be meeting up at her parents' house again the following day. Before this latest disaster, it had looked as if Tuesday lunch was going to become a ritual.

She wondered if Charlie had told his family about her treachery. If they weren't calling her, she'd have to call them. She couldn't just turn up at her parents' house tomorrow without checking. What if they didn't come? How would Meirah and Mike feel? What could she tell them? *Oh no*, she reflected. *If Mum finds out that James has been in my flat, she'll never forgive me either.* There followed a fresh bout of tears. Finally, she plucked up courage and phoned Gillian.

"You poor child. What happened?" Gillian wasn't condemning her at least.

"It was awful. James just turned up on the doorstep this morning. I couldn't turn him away. He said…"

By this time her words were incoherent, so Gillian interrupted her.

"Do you want me to drive over? Better you don't come here. Charlie jumped immediately to what I knew must be the wrong conclusion. He isn't fit company at the moment."

"Oh, would you, Gillian? I'd really like to be able to tell you my side of the story."

Once Gillian had arrived and was seated comfortably. Daisy began to relate the events of the morning. "So you see, I didn't really feel I had a choice," she finished.

"And you were right. What sort of a person would you be if you'd turned him away in that state? I know he'd have recovered quickly. I've lived with him for long enough. But you weren't to know that."

"But everyone will think I'm on his side."

"Not everyone."

Daisy didn't point out that by everyone she'd specifically meant Charlie. "I'm so glad you understand."

"I answered his call eventually, at about half past ten. He wanted to come and collect a few things and have a conversation. When I opened the door, he was already there. Apparently he'd just been waiting for me to pick up."

"What happened, if you don't mind me asking?"

"We talked about divorce. He wasn't particularly interested one way or the other. All he wants to know is that he's financially secure. I'll make an appointment to see a solicitor about the legalities, but in the meantime I've arranged to transfer a substantial amount to James's bank account — in instalments, so he doesn't blow it all once. After that was done, he had no reason to stay any longer. He didn't even say goodbye to the children. Kirsty was out and Charlie in his room with the door firmly closed. Still, under the circumstances it won't come as any surprise to you that they don't communicate."

"Is it all okay for tomorrow, then? Will I see you at Mum and Dad's?"

"Kirsty and I will be there. I can't answer for Charlie. I don't know why he's so mad, but it's riled him enough to decide it's time for his trip to Europe. From what I can understand, he's spent the day making travel arrangements. It looks like he'll probably be off before Kirsty, and she's going next week! I can't tell you how glad I am that you're still here."

Daisy wasn't to know the painful history that fuelled Charlie's need to get away. He'd been less than a year old when his mother had met and married James. A year before, his own father had been killed in a boating accident two months before Charlie was born. His earliest memory was of his stepfather turning away when he'd put out his chubby arms to be picked up. It never got any better, not even with James's own daughter. When Kirsty was born just after Charlie's fifth birthday, he became her champion. He'd idolised her from the moment her little fist had curled round his finger. That was his best early memory. As she'd grown up, he'd protected her from James's indifference. He'd made excuses: "He's busy, Kirsty. Come and play trains," or "He must be tired after working all day. I'll read you a bedtime story."

Later, when she was in her mid-teens, he'd warned her dates not to hurt her. She was happily settled with Cam now and planning a wedding next year. The only reason he hadn't come to the UK with them was because he was the CEO of what had been Gillian's business. Everything had happened so fast after James had dropped his bombshell about Meirah and Daisy, and Cam had too many commitments he couldn't rearrange at such short notice.

Charlie had nothing but contempt for James and had tolerated him only for his mother's sake. He was glad she'd finally thrown him out. It left him free to relinquish his self-imposed role as her protector and leave for his trip. Except he didn't really want to leave. He wanted to be near Daisy. But Daisy didn't want him, except as a brother, and now, what with this James business, he needed to put some distance between himself and his family. His contempt for his stepfather had festered over the years, but surely Daisy had even more reason to despise him? What had she been doing, serving him breakfast as cool as you please? At first he'd thought James had stayed the night. His mother had put him straight, but it still didn't explain why Daisy was entertaining the man who the night before had caused so much upset. No, better to leave and give himself time to think — something he definitely couldn't do when he was with the bubbly young woman to whom he'd lost his heart. What a bloody mess!

CHAPTER NINE

Charlie didn't come to Meirah and Mike's house the next day. The only communication Daisy had from him was a text message: *Have to get away. Need time to think. Take care.*

As they all sat down for lunch, Charlie was boarding the Eurostar on his way to Paris. By six o'clock French time, he was showered and dressed and on his way out to explore the city. Rumblings from inside reminded him he hadn't eaten since breakfast, so he found a charming brasserie hidden away in a small square near his hotel. The food was superb but he was reminded of the number of great meals he'd shared with Daisy and what he now felt was his enlarged family. Maybe Mike would teach him his way of cooking. Charlie was certainly willing to learn. But would it be best if he just went home, back to Australia? He could travel across Europe to the Far East, maybe as far as Hong Kong, and catch a plane from there. He had the time and the means. It would be an adventure. Somehow it didn't have much appeal. He'd be leaving too much behind. Ordering a brandy and a coffee, he decided to stay where he was for a while and investigate the splendour of the French capital while he searched for a solution to what seemed to be an insurmountable problem. Back in his room he lay on the bed with his fingers laced behind his head, looking for inspiration and finding none. Eventually he slept.

"I thought this was going to be my last lunch with you all. I booked my ticket for Monday, but I had a call from Cam just before we came out. I must say he sounded a bit tanked up."

"This early in the day?" Meirah gasped.

"No, Meirah," Kirsty said with a laugh. "It's evening over there."

"Of course. How stupid of me."

"Not at all. I can't get my head round it either. Anyway, it seems that everything is under control at home. He's feeling a bit left out, so he's managed to juggle his appointments and take the next three weeks off. He said, and I quote, 'It won't all be holiday, but I can get an awful lot done without actually having to be here.' He's sent me travel details and I've managed to put my booking back to coincide with his flight home. So it looks like you've got me for a while yet."

Everyone was pleased, of course, but none more so than Daisy, who was missing Charlie badly already. She'd been dreading Kirsty's imminent departure.

"That's fantastic news. He can come for lunch next Tuesday and fill Charlie's place."

"Thank you, Mike. He's not due to arrive until Sunday but he'd love to, I'm sure. I know he won't mind me speaking for him."

"And not even married yet! That bit's supposed to come later," Mike said, laughing.

Daisy managed to keep up appearances and even enjoyed the afternoon with her family, but later, when she was alone at home, she found herself wondering what Charlie was doing.

In the short time Charlie had been walking with her, Daisy had grown so used to him being there that in spite of her love for the dogs, something in her job had diminished. What made it worse was that with all three walks finished by lunchtime, she had the rest of the day to fill without him. She saw Gillian and Kirsty on Thursday, then drove to her parents' house on

Friday lunchtime. Thankfully Mike was home, as Meirah was completely absorbed in her latest painting and hidden away in her studio.

"What's the matter, kitten? You're looking a bit down in the mouth."

"No, I'm fine, Dad. Just one of those spring colds you get as soon as winter's over and you think you're safe." She could hardly tell him she was pining for her brother.

"I'm looking forward to meeting Cam on Tuesday. If he's like the rest of the family, it'll be delightful."

"He's not quite family yet, Dad."

"Speaking of which, have you heard from Charlie? I'd have thought he'd be in touch by now."

"Not a word. He's obviously far too busy having a good time chasing the French mademoiselles," she managed to reply without sounding bitter.

"Well, good luck to him. What else is a young man to do in Paris?"

Chasing the ladies was the last thing on Charlie's mind, unless Paris could be called a lady. He thought there must be few people on earth who would not be charmed by this beautiful city, but he wished Daisy was there to share it with him. Their taste in art was different, as they had discovered over the past couple of weeks. That wouldn't have stopped them enjoying perhaps the most famous painting in the world, the Mona Lisa, or admiring Venus de Milo and bemoaning the fact that her arms had never been recovered. He'd walked from the Louvre through the Tuileries, surely a garden for lovers, and along the Champs-Élysées to the Arc de Triomphe. Every time he saw a dog, he thought of Daisy, and as the French were very fond of their dogs he thought of her a lot. He'd spoken to his mother and sister a couple of times, but there'd been no word from Daisy. Scarcely remarkable, given his last message to her. *Have to get away*, he'd said. Hardly an invitation to talk. He was surprised therefore to see her name appear in his text notifications.

Hope you're having a good time, she'd written. *Oscar misses you. So do I.*

He almost shot off an immediate reply, but something held him back. He found a bench and sat down to think. There was no doubt in his mind how he felt about her. What he had to do was come to terms with the fact that she didn't feel the same. He had a big decision to make. Should he turn tail and run, or should he go back and be the brother Daisy wanted? He suspected the latter would be more painful, but didn't he also owe it to his mother to be there for her? Kirsty would be going back to Australia soon, and James was out of the picture. Gillian would be alone in England. She would have Daisy's family but, strong woman though she was, her son knew how much she would appreciate it if he stayed, for a while at least. He remembered the support she'd given him a couple of years back, when his own world had come crashing down around him.

"Come home, Charlie. You're always welcome here," she'd said.

He hadn't moved back in. It wasn't an option. For one thing, the sight of James turned his stomach. For another, he wouldn't have been able to tell his mother that, or why. She'd been there for him, though, as always, and now it was time for him to be there for her. He had to go back to London.

He picked up his phone to reply to Daisy: *Lovely to hear from you. Not the same without my personal tour guide. Coming home. Will text details of arrival.*

Charlie and Cam both arrived in London on Sunday. Though Daisy knew Charlie was in London, she could hardly go racing over to Wandsworth to see him. She still wasn't sure what her reception would be. She would never forget the look on Charlie's face the last time she'd seen him. Instead, after her Monday morning walks, she met Sam for lunch at a restaurant.

"You're never going to believe this," Sam said as soon as Daisy sat down.

"Try me."

"I've had my first scan, and I'm having twins!"

There was a pause in the conversation while Daisy took in the news.

"Oh great!" she protested drily. "They're going to cost me a bloody fortune."

"Too right. Niall and I want you to be their godmother." If anyone else in the restaurant wondered why two young women suddenly exploded with laughter, they were polite enough not to show it. "It's okay, though, Daisy. You can start saving straight away. Lunch is on me."

Daisy made her way to her parents' house the following day, where her entire family had gathered. Any discomfort she might have felt at seeing Charlie again vanished when she saw Gillian sitting in an armchair with her bandaged leg propped up on a stool.

"Gillian, what have you done?" she gasped.

Looking a bit embarrassed, Gillian explained that she'd had a bit of an argument with one of the pieces of the equipment at the gym. "No need, of course, to say who won. I was doing really well and heading for the next exercise when I tripped over and twisted my ankle. It's only sprained, I'm happy to say, but I feel so stupid."

"Come on, Mum, tell her the rest," Kirsty urged. When Gillian did not oblige, Kirsty went on, "She was rescued by a knight in shining armour."

"Actually, he was wearing a compression shirt and track pants," said Gillian with a laugh. "He insisted on taking me home, as I couldn't drive. He even insisted on coming with me to the hospital first in case my ankle was broken. Like I said, though, it's just twisted."

"And how old is he, this champion of yours?"

"Quite young, I think. Probably five or six years younger than me."

"You're not blushing, are you, Mum?" Charlie said, speaking for the first time since Daisy had arrived, giving her a chance at last to look at him directly.

"Of course not. It's just, well, you know what I'm like about my clothes. I'm uncomfortable sitting here with the leg of my beautiful trousers all scrunched up. They'll never be the same."

"What did they say at the hospital?" Meirah asked. "Is it a six-week job?"

"No, it's an elasticated bandage, not a cast. But I'm supposed to keep off the leg for a while. Lucky it's on my left side. The car's an automatic, so at least I'll be able to drive. Mind you, I was grateful to have Charlie back to bring us over today. Cam's still too jetlagged to get behind the wheel of a car. I can't think why you never learned to drive, Kirsty."

"Never had the need, really, although Cam says he's going to teach me when we get home." She turned to her fiancé and introduced him to Daisy, whom he hugged as if she were an old friend.

"After all, you are going to be my sister-in-law."

"And you'd better make sure you look after Kirsty or you'll have me to answer to, even if I have to come all the way to Australia."

"Great idea. You'll come for the wedding anyway, won't you? All of you?"

"Sounds like a plan to me," said Mike. "Now, table everyone, please. Lunch is ready. I'll leave the seating arrangements to you. Daisy, take the footstool in for Gillian, please. Meirah, love, you've got paint on your nose."

Lunch followed the usual routine of everyone talking at once. Charlie regaled them all with an account of his trip to Paris, while Cam told them about the stress of a five-hour delay in Hong Kong. "I've been there before. All I could think about was the time I was wasting sitting in an airport lounge when I could have been out on the town."

"Oh, that was all, was it?" Kirsty quipped.

"Of course not, Kirsty. I was desperate to see you, sweetheart, but if I had to wait I'd far rather have been diverted in a bustling city than staring at a lot of chrome and glass. It just made the waiting longer."

"Nice recovery," Mike and Charlie said in unison.

"Trust you men to stick together," Daisy said. "Is anyone topping up the wine? My glass is empty."

Charlie picked up the bottle and walked around the table, filling glasses as he went. He brushed against Daisy as he leaned past her, spilling a little on the tablecloth in the process.

"What a waste," he said, putting his hand on her shoulder by way of an apology. "If Mum doesn't need me, would you like company walking the dogs tomorrow, Daisy? I want to see if there's any truth in the rumour that Oscar's been pining for me."

"Go ahead, Charlie. I think Kirsty and Cam would like some time together. As a seasoned tourist, she's going to show him some of the things she's seen so far and I'm going to stay in with my feet up. I've spent hardly any time at home since we arrived."

Meirah looked across the table at Gillian. "You've gone all red again. Do you feel okay? Is the ankle giving you pain? It isn't like you to stay at home when there are things to do and places to see."

"Brian said he might drop by to see how I am."

"Brian?"

"Erm, my knight in shining armour."

There were a few moments of uncomfortable silence before Daisy stepped into the breach, casting back to Charlie's original question. "Of course it's true, Charlie. Oscar and I would both love you to come."

CHAPTER TEN

"Have we got time for a quick coffee before we go?" said Charlie when he turned up on Daisy's doorstep the next morning. "There's something I need to tell you."

"Of course," Daisy said, though her heart was pounding so loudly she was sure he'd be able to hear. "Come into the kitchen while I make it."

Facing her across the room and cradling the mug in his hands, he looked as if he didn't know where to begin.

"We can leave it if you're not ready," she said, though by now she was desperate to know what was wrong.

He sat back, and she could see the effort he made to relax.

"No, it's fine. It's about James," he said at last. "It's obvious I was pretty upset the other day when I found him here. It threw me off my stride completely and I blamed you. That's not how it should be. I know brothers and sisters squabble when they're little — we missed that bit, of course — but as grown-ups we should be there for each other, and I wasn't there for you, Daisy. I didn't even give you a chance to explain. I've been wanting to say sorry ever since."

"I can see how it must have looked, Charlie, but it wasn't like that at all. He just turned up on the doorstep, saying he'd slept on a park bench of all things. He looked awful and told me Gillian wasn't answering his calls. I gave him breakfast then threw him out. I told him I didn't want to see him again."

"If that's true, I can tell you why it affected me so much." He took a deep breath. "It happened a couple of years ago. I had a girlfriend. She was more than that. We were living together. Trying each other on for size, I suppose you could say, though I'm not sure either of us thought it would all end happily ever after."

Daisy tried very hard not to be jealous.

"It's the old story. I came home early one day and found them together."

"Them?"

"My girlfriend and James."

"What!"

"I don't think Mum's had any illusions for a long time now. Even you must have seen how charming he can be when he wants to. He was always flitting from one woman to another, but I don't think Mum ever knew any of them. I'm not sure what she'd have done if I'd told her it was in our own backyard! Maybe she'd have left him sooner, and maybe that would have been a good thing, but I didn't and she must never know. I was gutted at the time, as you can imagine. She was an absolute rock when my ex and I broke up. She even asked if I'd like to move back home. Hah! What a joke that would have been, playing happy families."

"Charlie, I'm so sorry."

"It's okay. Like I said, I don't think it would have been permanent. It was just the feeling of betrayal, so much more from him than from her. I can only think of him with loathing now, but I hope it explains why I reacted so harshly that morning. I'm sorry."

"You have nothing to be sorry about, other than the fact that you went to Paris without me," Daisy said, hoping to lighten the mood.

"That was definitely a mistake. I did tell you it wasn't the same without my personal guide. We'll have to go together next time."

She liked the sound of that. "Okay. In the meantime, there is a rather large dog who I think will be more than a little excited when he sees you. Prepare to square your shoulders. I take absolutely no responsibility for his actions."

She was quite right. When they got to Oscar's house, Charlie planted his feet squarely on the ground and braced himself. Just as well. Oscar launched himself at him as if he'd been gone for weeks instead of days. Charlie was hardly less delighted.

After the morning walks had been completed and Charlie had hurried home to check on Gillian, Daisy received a phone call. It was Sam.

"What are you doing on the twenty-first?" Sam asked.

"Is this a trick question?"

"Talk about suspicious. No. Are you free?"

"When? Morning, afternoon or evening?"

"All of them."

"Okay, now I know something's up. I don't trust you when you're in this mood. I'm not committing myself to anything until I know what it is."

"I'm getting married. I'm getting MARRIED."

"Bloody hell, that's brilliant! Of course I'm free."

"That's good, because I want you to be my maid of honour. Not only that, but I haven't got a dress yet."

"When are your parents due back from New York?"

"They fly home the Tuesday before. They don't even go until tomorrow, and of course Mum wanted to cancel when I told her but no way would I let them do that. They've been saving up since forever. It's supposed to be their holiday of a lifetime."

"What will you do for the wedding reception?"

"Something small. Just immediate family and very close friends. Niall's parents will be flying in the day before as well, so it's just you and me, Daisy."

"And why this unseemly haste, as if I didn't know?"

"It's not me. It's Niall. 'No children of mine are going to be born out of wedlock,' he said. Out of wedlock! It could have been my grandfather talking! So I told him, 'If we're going to be married before the babies come, we're going to be married before they show.'"

"So, what's it to be? A white wedding? The full works?"

"With your help, yes. Are you up for it?"

"You bet. When can we start?"

"Is tomorrow too soon?"

"What about work?"

"Lunch hours this week and next. Then I'll be on leave until after the wedding and we'll really be able to go for it."

"In the meantime, I'll start organising your hen party."

"Don't be silly. It's not necessary, and in any case there isn't time."

"Don't be daft, of course you must have a hen do. Every bride should. It's a rite of passage."

"Okay, but if you do anything crazy, I'll never forgive you."

"As if I would. All you have to do is be at the right place at the designated time. I'll let you know when and where as soon as I can. After all, I've got a whole two and a half weeks at my disposal."

Meirah offered her home for the hen do and Daisy sent the invites the following day. Sam had specifically asked that Gillian and Kirsty be there, along with a friend from work and two women she and Daisy had been friends with since school. Daisy sent the details to Sam's mother in a text. Mike would cater the small party and then make himself scarce.

"We can't throw you out of your own home, Dad," said Daisy.

"You're not. It's just that I have a strong sense of self-preservation, and I'm not prepared to put myself at the mercy of that many women."

The next couple of weeks flew by in a whirl of activity. Sam's enthusiasm was delightful. It seemed her only major concern was that her bump shouldn't be visible on her wedding day. This fear was laid to rest when they found the perfect dress on only their third outing. It was Jane Austen style with a fitted bustline, below which the soft ivory material fell away from the body in delicate folds.

"It's amazing, Sam. You look beautiful."

Sam looked at her reflection in the mirror and a smile transformed her face. "This is the one, isn't it?"

"Absolutely."

"Okay, your turn now."

Daisy tried on several bridesmaid dresses and, as with Sam, the mirror told her when she'd found the right one. A floor-length chiffon dress in sage, it complemented Daisy's colouring and accentuated the green flecks in her hazel eyes.

"It's perfect. Dresses sorted. What's next on the agenda?"

"Shoes. White satin for you, and I'll have mine dyed to match the dress. It'll be nice to wear something other than trainers for a change. Do you want to carry a little bag, Sam, or just a bouquet?"

"I suppose I'd better have something to keep a hankie in, just in case I cry or, much more likely, I have to pass it to my mother, who most certainly will."

During their daily walks, Daisy kept Charlie up to date with all the arrangements. He was seeing less of her because so much of her time was devoted to her friend. Maybe it was for the best. It was hard maintaining his brotherly role, but somehow they'd managed to settle into a pattern of behaviour that didn't seem to threaten Daisy's peace of mind.

There were times when Charlie was at a bit of a loss. Kirsty and Cam were spending as much time alone together as they could. Gillian had several times decided to stay at home, citing her injury as the reason, but no-one was fooled: she was spending more and more time with Brian. Left to his own devices, her son spent several afternoons being a tourist. He loved London.

As the wedding day approached, so did the time for Kirsty and Cam to return to Australia. Daisy was having difficulty dealing with it, as was Kirsty. On the day of Sam's hen do, they stood together in Meirah and Mike's kitchen, washing some of the dirty glasses.

"Promise me, absolutely promise me you'll come over for the wedding next year, Daisy. I couldn't bear to lose you now."

Daisy tried to lighten the mood before they both dissolved into tears. "If you think I'm going to miss *your* hen party, never mind the big day, you can think again. Of course I'll be there."

The noise from the sitting room was reaching hazardous proportions.

"I know now why Dad decided to go out," said Daisy. "And it's going to get worse. We haven't eaten yet and we've got Pictionary to do first. Come on, let's get these glasses back in there and filled up."

There were a dozen women of varying ages in the other room. Daisy, as chief organiser, stood on a chair, trying to get everyone's attention. It wasn't working, so Kirsty put two fingers in her mouth and whistled, shocking the ladies into silence.

"Pictionary time, girls," Daisy announced. "Split yourselves into two teams. Here, Kirsty, pass the pads and pencils around, please. I'll go first just to start the ball rolling. The first person who gets it wins the point for their team and takes the next slot. There are plenty of ideas in this little box. Just pick one at random."

"Oh no! I hate party games," Sam wailed.

"Of course you don't, Sam. I've known you too long for you to try and pull that one. Anyway, this is as crazy as it gets. I promised, remember."

Daisy squiggled for a while until she'd produced something that was just about recognisable as a figure.

"I get it. You've got your hands clasped in front of you. It's you, Sam, at the altar, taking your vows."

"Wrong. Sorry, Gillian."

There were no other offers, so Daisy scribbled a bit more. This time the head was turned. It looked as if it was going to fall off.

"You're hopeless, you lot. Okay, one more try."

This time she added the giveaway and they all shouted at once.

"Tossing the bouquet!"

"At last! Right, I think you were loudest, Jen. Here, pick a card," Daisy said, handing the box to Sam's mum. "Oh, and I forgot to mention that you only have sixty seconds from start to finish."

Chaos descended until they all fell back exhausted from laughing.

"Time to eat. Dining room, everyone," Meirah said. "This way."

Mike had done them proud. Once they'd eaten their fill, they went back into the other room for the final part of the celebrations. Daisy had sneaked out when everyone was eating and piled all the presents onto the coffee table. Sam was hugely embarrassed.

"There weren't supposed to be any presents. You shouldn't have."

"Nonsense," said her mother, and that was the end of it. Sam sat on the floor, not knowing where to start. She picked up the parcel nearest to her, and inside she found a spa voucher.

"What a great idea, Gillian, thank you. It's perfect."

Sam picked up another small package. It was from her work friend and contained a blue and white garter. "For the wedding — something blue," she said unnecessarily.

"It's beautiful. I love it."

Daisy had given Sam the kind of lacy lingerie you always want but can never justify buying for yourself. After opening all the rest, Sam finally came to the last present. It was a book from her mother: *Inter Course: An Aphrodisiac's Cookbook*.

"Oh, Mum! How could you?" Sam laughed.

"Well, I know how you love cooking. This will just make it easier to rustle something up," her mother replied archly.

It was the end of a wonderful party, and Sam gave Daisy the biggest hug before piling all her gifts into the back of a cab.

"Go on then, bugger off," said Daisy with a giggle. "Leave me to do all the clearing up. I don't mind."

"Meirah, I don't know how you put up with her," Sam retorted. "Please thank Mike for all the lovely food. See you on Saturday. Bye."

CHAPTER ELEVEN

On Friday evening, Daisy's family had a small dinner party which for once wasn't catered by Mike. Gillian had been told about a wonderful restaurant where the food was supposed to be amazing and there was a small dancefloor for the more energetic customers. This would be the last sensible opportunity for them all to get together. Kirsty and Cam were leaving in the early hours of Monday morning.

Gillian had decided to invite Brian, and everyone was eager to meet him. It was difficult to be subtle when they wanted to know so much more about him, so Charlie came straight to the point.

"You've been great to Mum since she hurt her ankle, and we know you've been seeing a lot of her. We were just wondering, have you been avoiding us?"

Brian looked a bit sheepishly at Gillian, and there was no doubting the warmth in the look she gave him.

"You have to blame your mother there. I've been plaguing her to introduce me for some time now, but she's been a bit reticent. I think she's not sure you'll approve," he said, covering her hand with his.

"What's not to approve? You're both adults. If you like each other, it's nothing to do with anyone else, even us."

"Yes, and I'm sure you know enough about the family to know my father is out of the picture," Kirsty added. "It's nice for *me* to know that someone other than Charlie is looking out for Mum now I'm going home."

"I'm certainly doing my best, Kirsty. I understand that Sam and Niall have asked if I'll come to the wedding tomorrow. If it's okay with you all, I'd love to, but I don't want to step on any toes."

"Particularly not Mum's. Her foot's not quite better yet, you know."

"Thank you, Kirsty, and you too Charlie. Now, if you've all finished talking about me as if I weren't here, perhaps we could move on to the next course," Gillian huffed.

Spring had certainly arrived and Sam looked as if she too was blossoming. The dress was doing the job every wedding gown should do. Her mother, Jen, was wearing a pink knee-length dress with a matching coat, which by lucky chance complemented Aileen's navy and white. Having sensibly made sure that both mothers had been supplied with a square of white linen, Sam was led into the registry office by her father, where the small bridal party was waiting. As the strains of the 'Bridal Chorus' accompanied her entrance, two hankies were discreetly withdrawn from their hiding places. Niall looked as if he would burst with pride. The little procession made its way down the aisle and Daisy came into view. Charlie managed to smother his gasp with a spontaneous fit of coughing. She was looking stunning. While everyone else had eyes only for the bride, Charlie's gaze was constantly on Daisy.

At a cue from the registrar, the best man, Sean, took a small box from his pocket, rings were exchanged and the deed was done. There was a short speech from the officiant, who spoke to them as if to old friends, and then they all went to a local function room where a buffet lunch was waiting for them. The bride and groom faced their guests from a long table, their parents on either side. Six round tables horseshoed a small dancefloor. The festivities began. Delivering his speech, Sean paid fulsome compliments to his friend and related many incidents from their youth which embarrassed or amused Niall in varying degrees.

"And do you remember when…"

"That's enough, Sean. It's my turn now," Niall said, rising to his feet. "I'd like to begin by welcoming you all here today to help celebrate our wedding. There won't be any amongst you who don't know that Sam is pregnant. She has already made me happier than I could have believed possible. I'd like you all to raise your glasses and drink a toast to my beautiful wife and the mother of my children." He turned from his audience to face her. "Darlin' girl, I love you with all my heart." He raised his glass. "To Sam."

"To Sam," rang around the room.

After the wedding, Charlie and Kirsty returned to Wandsworth and sat up late, discussing their mother's relationship with Brian. Gillian had gone straight to bed, as her ankle was bothering her. At Brian's insistence they'd taken to the floor for a couple of slow dances, and though he'd borne most of her weight, almost lifting her off her feet, she'd been reminded of her recent injury when a niggling ache turned to pain.

"Did you see them dancing? He must be every bit as fit as he looks. I'm not sure Mum was keen, though, and with good reason," said Charlie. "She definitely had a little furrow between her eyes when she went upstairs just now."

"He's obviously crazy about her, Charlie. I'm sure he was just using the music as an excuse to be close to her. Haven't you ever been in love?" Kirsty shut her mouth quickly, remembering what her brother had been through. He'd confided in her about James's betrayal.

"Well, you'd have needed a chisel to prise them apart this evening," he said, ignoring the question. "Still, if Mum's happy then I am too. Particularly as you're off home. I know he's your father, Kirsty, but when I think of what James has done to her, I could almost kill him. It's nice to know someone is looking out for her, apart from us."

Charlie had misgivings about Brian, but there was no point in laying them on his sister when she wasn't going to be here. At least that was something he could talk to Daisy about — he'd value her thoughts on the subject. Maybe he was being overly protective.

CHAPTER TWELVE

Daisy arrived in Wandsworth at midday on Sunday. She'd been asked to join the family for a final lunch before Kirsty and Cam's departure. The intention had been to go to a local restaurant, but Gillian's ankle was still bothering her, so they decided to get a takeaway instead. Kirsty and Cam were busy sorting out travel documents and doing some last-minute packing while Daisy and Charlie pored over the menu card, which was already covered in ticks.

"I can't believe you've been in England long enough to have mutilated this so badly."

"We're all fans. I hope you like Indian food."

"Love it. Trouble is, there's always so much choice I end up eating far more than is good for me."

Charlie laughed and pretended to whisk the menu away from her. Daisy tried to give him a playful punch in the stomach, but he was ready for her and grabbed her wrist. Even that small touch sent sparks flying between them. He dropped her wrist and picked up the menu, then looked around for a pen and notepad.

"We can order as much as we like, then if there's anything left over we can have it for lunch after we've walked the dogs tomorrow," Daisy suggested.

"Wonderful! I love leftovers."

Daisy's face dropped and she fell silent.

"What? What's the matter?"

"They'll be gone. By the time we have lunch tomorrow, Kirsty and Cam will be in the air." She looked at Charlie, instantly subdued. "I'm going to miss her so much, Charlie. I feel like a child who's been given the best Christmas present ever and then had it taken away again."

"We'll go over for the wedding, I promise. In the meantime, won't I do? I'm going to miss her too, remember. So will Mum, even with Brian around."

When the food came, the mood at the table was mixed. It was fun, no doubt about it, but tinged with sadness too. They managed to make the feast last for most of the day, but the party broke up mid-evening as Kirsty and Cam had an early start the next morning.

"Daisy, can you just come and check my hand luggage with me in case I've forgotten something?" Kirsty asked.

Daisy followed her sister upstairs and was surprised to see a tiny parcel tied with a pink ribbon sitting on top of Kirsty's case.

"It's for you," she said.

"Oh, but I haven't... I didn't..."

"This isn't an exchange. It's something I want you to have. Please open it now, while I'm still here."

Daisy sat on the bed, Kirsty next to her, as she pulled the ribbon away and removed the paper to find a small box. Inside was a tiny silver bracelet, the kind that was given to a new baby. There was no way an adult could have worn it, and Daisy knew this was a memento from Kirsty's childhood. Her voice was a bit choked as she said, "I can't, Kirsty. It's yours. I couldn't possibly."

"I would be very hurt if you didn't accept it. I brought it halfway across the world for you."

"But you didn't know me. You didn't even know if you'd like me."

"Too right. That's why you're getting it now, and not when we first met."

"I don't know what to say."

"Just remember me every time you look at it. I don't want you to forget me."

"As if I could. But it was given to you."

"Yes, by Mummy, and I asked her permission before we left Oz. There's something more than the links in this chain that bind us, Daisy, but in case you ever need reminding, the bracelet will be there."

The two girls hugged long and hard, and not long after they went back downstairs Daisy drove home with a lump in her throat and a warm feeling in her heart.

Daisy felt particularly low on Monday morning, and even Charlie's company didn't help lift her spirits. By the time they'd settled Muffin at home and got back to Daisy's flat, it was obvious to both of them that this was more than just a reaction to Kirsty and Cam's departure.

"But I'm never ill," said Daisy.

"You are now."

"What can I do? What about the dogs?"

"The first thing you can do is make an appointment to see the doctor. The second is to take yourself off to bed until it's time to see him. We'll get a cab there. Now, make that phone call. You're as white as a ghost."

Daisy couldn't face lunch, and as the leftovers from the previous day were back in Wandsworth Charlie raided her fridge while she went to bed. He followed her into the room, carrying a cup of tea and her mobile.

"Do you think you can manage to phone, just to see if it's okay for me to have the keys from tomorrow onwards and take the dogs out on my own for the time being? I don't think you'll be doing any walking for a while."

Daisy made the calls and there was no problem. Charlie had been walking the dogs with her for long enough now, and all the owners were only too pleased that there was a solution. That done, Charlie pulled the curtains to shut out the light and left her in peace. Taking a book off the shelf in the sitting room, he settled down to wait, but when he went to rouse Daisy it was obvious she was in no fit state to go anywhere. He didn't want to wake her, so he guiltily scrolled through the contacts on her phone. At least the doctor was near the top. Charlie asked the receptionist if Daisy could have a home visit, and she promised the doctor would call in after surgery that evening. An hour later, Daisy, who had woken and realised she'd missed her appointment, appeared in the doorway in a panic and then fainted before Charlie could catch her. He lifted her tenderly and carried her back to bed. Then he went back to the kitchen for a glass of water. She was conscious again, so he told her about the change of plan and managed to get her to drink a few sips before she raised her hand weakly in protest. Laying her gently back on the pillow, he went out, leaving the door open in case she should call. He phoned Gillian.

"I'm sorry, Mum. I don't really want to leave you on your own today of all days, but I'm going to have to stay and look after Daisy. She's come down with something and I've called the doctor. I'll check with Meirah first to see if she wants to come, but I thought I should let you know."

"Don't worry, Charlie. Brian's coming over this evening anyway. It's not a problem."

"Okay, I'll get back to you later. After the doctor's been."

It was while he was waiting for Meirah to answer that he remembered she and Mike had gone to stay with friends somewhere in Surrey and wouldn't be back until the following

Saturday, so instead of having the conversation he'd intended he just reassured her that Daisy would be fine.

"I thought you'd want to know, but don't worry, I'll stay with her until she's fit enough to look after herself or until she gets so fed up with me that she throws me out."

Meirah was satisfied that things couldn't be too bad if Charlie was making a joke, but he was glad she couldn't see just how bad Daisy looked. She'd probably have come running home.

Charlie could hear Daisy moaning from time to time and kept leaping up to look in on her, but the noises she was making were coming from her unconscious state. At seven o'clock, he jumped up to let the doctor in.

"Am I pleased to see you. I've made her as comfortable as possible, but I didn't know what else to do. She's in here," Charlie said, leading the way. He left the room, closing the door behind him, and waited anxiously until the examination was complete.

"It's a very nasty bout of flu. She should be fine with rest and care. Unfortunately there isn't too much we can do for her. Make sure she has plenty of fluids. She can have paracetamol if she's feverish or achy. Apart from that, it's just a matter of time. Call me again if you need to, but it probably won't be necessary. Just keep her quiet and as comfortable as possible."

"Thank you, Doctor, and thanks for coming round."

"She might suffer from loss of appetite as well. Don't worry about it. Just be sensible and don't present her with a three-course meal. Oh, and you might like to get her into a nightie as well. She's a bit restricted with her jeans on."

"I will. Goodnight."

"Goodnight."

Get her into a nightie! How on earth am I going to do that? Charlie thought. *Ah well, if she really thinks of me as a brother, it shouldn't worry her too much.*

Taking a deep breath, Charlie set about removing Daisy's jeans. She began to struggle and punched him in the eye. He realised she didn't know it was him and was probably imaging all sorts of things.

"Daisy, it's me, Charlie. The doctor said I was to get you into your nightie. Just lie still while I get you undressed. I promise to look the other way."

He was relieved to see comprehension in her eyes. She relaxed just enough for him to help her.

"I'm just going to get you a honey and lemon drink. The doctor said you have a bad case of flu, so just for once you're going to have to let somebody else look after you. I'll be back in a minute," he said, tucking the duvet under her chin. When he returned with the drink a few minutes later, she was fast asleep.

Feeling he'd done as much as he could, Charlie phoned for a takeaway and opened a bottle of wine. He switched on the TV, turned off the sound and went for the subtitles instead, to ensure he wouldn't drown out any sounds from the bedroom.

In the meantime, his meal was delivered and he went into the bathroom to wash his hands, only to be shocked by the vision that stared back at him from the mirror. His features were somewhat distorted by the swelling around his left eye, and signs of bruising were already apparent. Charlie touched it gingerly with the tips of his fingers.

As the night wore on, it became obvious that Daisy was becoming worse. The constant moans and little noises worried him. Three or four times he managed to persuade her to take a few sips of water and, once, some paracetamol. Otherwise, there was little he could do for her. Also on his mind was the fact that he'd have to leave in the morning to walk the dogs. It would take a minimum of three hours. He'd be able to pop back in between walks to check up on Daisy, but he wouldn't be able to stay long because he'd learned by now how important routine was to Oscar and the rest.

CHAPTER THIRTEEN

Charlie's eye was almost completely shut by morning and Daisy, awake at last, wondered if he'd walked into a door.

"No, it was your fist."

"Don't be silly. I wouldn't do that to you."

"Let me tell you, you would and you did, and you pack a fine punch," he said, leaning over to feel her forehead. "I'm going to scramble an egg for you before I go to Oscar's. Do you think you could manage that?"

"I feel awful."

"Wrong answer. Just have a bit and keep sipping that honey and lemon. Then you can go back to sleep."

Daisy sank into the pillows, closing her eyes then flicking them open again. "Why did I punch you in the eye?"

"I'll tell you later. Get some more rest while I make your breakfast."

The morning was uneventful and Charlie, having checked on Daisy twice, got back to the flat at lunchtime to find her fast asleep. Her cheeks were very red and he could see she was restless. He made another honey and lemon drink, another scrambled egg and half a slice of bread. Waking her gently, he waited while she took a couple of tablets then left her to sleep again and went home to get some clothes. On the way he called Meirah to give her an update and reassure her that Daisy was making progress. He opened the lounge door of the Wandsworth house to find his mother and Brian in a compromising position. Enjoying their embarrassment, he said, "It's all right. I've just come to collect a few things then I'll leave you in peace." He had a good chuckle. At least Gillian wasn't sitting around, pining for him or Kirsty. "Is it all right if I borrow the car, Mum?" He couldn't resist adding, "You don't look like you'll be needing it for a while."

He drove back to Blackheath, where he found Daisy still asleep. As it was a lovely day, he opened the window a tiny bit to let some fresh air in. Daisy stirred. It broke his heart to see her looking so poorly. He sat on the edge of her bed, deciding he could serve her best by being matter-of-fact rather than overly sympathetic.

"I'm going to do some shopping. I thought I'd get some ready-made soups and some yoghurt. Is there anything else you'd like? Some soft fruit, maybe?"

He was horrified to see tears pouring down her cheeks.

"What's the matter, Daisy?"

"You're being so nice to me."

"Meaning I'm not usually nice to you?"

"Meaning I remembered how you got the black eye. It's looking quite spectacular, you know."

"I forgive you if you forgive me. I didn't really have any choice. I promise to forget everything I saw."

"Don't leave me, Charlie. I don't think I can look after myself at the moment."

"I wouldn't dream of it. Well, only to get some shopping and to walk the dogs. They do come first, you know, even before you."

"Were they okay this morning?"

"They were fine." He could see that even this short conversation was taxing what little strength she had, so he stood up, turning at the door to ask, "By the way, do you have a spare duvet and pillows? It was very uncomfortable on the couch last night."

"You didn't open it? It's a sofa-bed. A good one too. The spare bedding is in that cupboard over there," she said, pointing to the top of one of the wardrobes.

Charlie couldn't believe he hadn't thought to look. "I'll get that stuff down later. In the meantime, I'm off. Try and get some more sleep. I'll be back soon with some goodies to tempt your delicate palate."

An hour later Charlie was back in the kitchen, unpacking the shopping. His phone rang twice. The first time it was Meirah, checking to see how her daughter was.

"Definitely a bit better. Certainly nothing to worry about," he said, though he was still worried himself at how pale and wan Daisy was. "How's Mike? Are you having a good time? Great. I'll call if there's any change."

As he put his mobile down on the worktop, his mother's name appeared on the display.

"Hello, Mum. How's the ankle?"

"It's on the mend, thank you."

"Must be all that physiotherapy."

"Don't be cheeky."

"I didn't mean to be. You're a grown woman and you know how I feel about James. I'm just glad that you've broken away at last. It's time you enjoyed yourself for a change."

"You make me sound pathetic. I always enjoyed work, you know."

"It's not quite the same, though, is it?"

"Okay. Change of subject. How's Daisy?"

"Not as good as I'd like but better than she was, I think. At least I can take away the burden of worrying about dogs. I wouldn't be surprised if she dragged herself out of bed if I wasn't here to take them out. Not that I think she'd make it as far as the front door."

"She's that poorly?"

"Just very weak. Are you okay for this evening?"

"I am being very well looked after. In every way."

"Mother! I'm shocked!"

"It'd take a lot more than that to shock you, son. Talk to you tomorrow. Give my love to Daisy. Night."

"Night."

Charlie popped his head round the bedroom door to hear Daisy snoring gently. He'd enjoy teasing her about that when she got better. He began preparing supper, the same for them both, as he was hoping that if they ate together she might be encouraged to eat more. He was concerned too that she wasn't having enough fluids and decided that the time had come for a bit of gentle bullying. She opened her eyes when he went in.

"Oh crap, you look awful!" she exclaimed.

"Not the best welcome I've ever had."

"Have you looked in the mirror?"

He went to inspect his reflection. "What have you done to me? I thought I got a few funny looks when I was out shopping. Now I know why."

Varying shades of brown and yellow adorned his face as the bruise worked its way out from his eye.

"Just wait until you're better. I'll be planning my revenge. In the meantime, is it okay if I eat in here with you? That way, we might at least have some conversation before you drop off again."

On Wednesday morning, Daisy was sitting up in bed when Charlie took her breakfast in.

"Well, that's a good sign. How do you feel?"

"Weak and wobbly, but I slept right the way through. Now I'm dying for a shower."

"Do you think you could wait until after I've walked the dogs? I think I should be here."

Daisy looked a bit alarmed.

"Not to scrub your back. It's just that you are still very weak and, not to put too fine a point on it, you've been feverish and sweating a lot. If you can hang on, I'll change the bed linen while you shower and then I can tuck you back in. You may not realise just how fragile you are."

"I don't know how I could have managed without you these last few days, Charlie."

"I know. I'm wonderful, aren't I? Now eat your breakfast and while I'm gone, if you're up to it, phone your mother. I'm sure she'll feel better if she hears your voice rather than mine."

"Just kiss the top of Oscar's head for me, will you? And let Muffin give you a big lick. As for the twins, tell them I'm missing them and I'll be back as soon as I can."

"I will. I'm pleased to see you've got your appetite back. You've done really well this morning. Do you want me to bring you a book, or are you going back to sleep?"

"I think maybe sleep. Just eating and talking to you has taken it out of me."

"It's all this intellectual conversation. Very tiring. Lie down then. Do you want the curtains open?"

"Yes please. The sunshine is glorious. It would be a shame to shut it out, and I don't think anything will keep me awake at the moment."

He handed her the phone.

"Don't forget to phone Meirah."

Charlie had a great time walking the dogs. He even attempted a couple of obedience exercises with Oscar, but the huge Bernese didn't have time for that sort of thing. There were much more important things to do. In the end, Charlie decided he would have to be content with having mastered Oscar's desire to drag him along the street. George and Mildred were as ever a delight, and he thought that as it was Thursday the next day, he might take them back to the flat for a little while to cheer Daisy up, if she was well enough. Since the dry weather had set in, Muffin didn't need a bath. Truth to tell, Charlie was a bit disappointed, but he did get the obligatory lick from chin to nose. It brought on a bout of sneezing, but he didn't care. He loved the dogs as much as Daisy did, and by now an idea was beginning to form. It would have to wait for the time being, though, certainly until Daisy was well and truly better.

By the time he got back to the flat, Charlie was feeling really good and hoping Daisy's improvement had continued throughout the morning. When he opened the door, he was surprised to hear voices coming from the bedroom, and even more so when he went through to find a man he'd never seen before sitting on the end of the bed. Daisy was looking paler than he'd have liked. He raised an eyebrow at her.

"Charlie, this is Jonathan. An old friend. Jonathan, Charlie."

"A bit more than an old friend," Jonathan smiled in a proprietary way Charlie didn't like at all and stood up to shake hands with him. "You're Daisy's long-lost brother, I understand."

"That's right. And you're…" He left the question hanging.

"Ex-boyfriend, but hoping to persuade Daisy to drop the ex. That's quite a shiner you've got there. Been in a fight?"

"Only with Daisy, but I aim to get my revenge. Have you been here long?"

"About an hour, I think. I nearly went away when I didn't get an answer after the first two rings, but eventually Daisy dragged herself to the door to let me in."

"How did you know she was here? Normally she'd be working at this time."

"I didn't. I was in the area and thought I'd give it a try."

Charlie didn't believe him for one moment. He caught Daisy looking despairingly at him behind Jonathan's back and decided to take charge.

"Well, I think perhaps it's time we let her rest. She's looking exhausted. I'm going to have some coffee. Would you like one before you go?"

"Thank you, but no. I'll be off then," he said, turning back to Daisy and kissing the top of her head. Everything in Charlie's body tightened with jealousy. "I'll come back again soon."

Charlie showed Jonathan out. He'd disliked him on sight but had to admit that was probably due to the circumstances. If this was what Daisy wanted, he was going to make damn sure she was treated properly. Having accepted that she regarded *him* only as a brother, he'd make sure everyone else would go through a rigorous process of examination before he'd let them get to her. All his pleasure in the morning had gone, and he went back into the bedroom with a heavy heart. He forced a smile to his face.

"Entertaining men in your bedroom behind my back, eh?"

"You don't know how pleased I was to see you come through the door. My poor head is spinning. He doesn't know when to stop talking."

That sounded promising.

"Well, I do. Honey and lemon and then back to sleep for you."

"Oh no, Charlie."

"A mutiny?"

"No, but do you think I could have a cup of tea?"

"Coming right away. Then you really must sleep. The dogs were fine, by the way."

When he returned a few minutes later with the tea, she was already fast asleep. He'd make a fresh one as soon as she woke up again.

CHAPTER FOURTEEN

This was an entirely new situation for Charlie. Not only could he not pursue the woman he loved, but he felt bound to advance someone else's cause in order to make her happy. He knew he felt antagonistic towards Jonathan purely out of jealousy, but he still felt justified in phoning him when he had no more sense than to call Daisy and wake her up.

"Hi, Jonathan. It's Charlie. I wonder if you'd mind using my number so as not to disturb Daisy. She's quite fretful now and finding it difficult to get back to sleep. I can always pass you over if she's awake."

To his credit, Jonathan was full of remorse. "Yes, of course. Stupid of me. I just want to ... now that I'm in touch again. Well, I'm sure you understand. What was that number?"

He'd said all the right things, but Charlie couldn't see what Daisy saw in him. He seemed so upright and English and pompous.

Daisy ventured out of the bedroom for an hour late in the afternoon. She was very weak and wobbly, but sick of staring at the four walls. Charlie, glad of her company, shuffled up and they spent a companionable hour sitting on the sofa watching the TV. He'd got up after a few moments to make her a cup of tea, and the relish with which she drank it was a sign she was on the mend. She tired fairly quickly so he ordered her back to her room with the promise of a sumptuous feast if she promised to be good and have a sleep first. She submitted readily. He'd wanted to talk to her about Jonathan and find out how strong her feelings were for him. In the very short time Charlie had spent with him, he'd come to the conclusion that

Jonathan was a nice enough guy but lacking a sense of the ridiculous, something Charlie was certain would be an essential part of any lasting relationship with Daisy.

The sumptuous feast was carrot and coriander soup followed by a plain omelette. Daisy joined Charlie at the table and did justice to his offering, though even that exhausted her. She sat with him for a while, but she looked so peaky that he packed her off to bed again, telling her he was going out for a while and promising to make another cup of tea when he got back.

Charlie drove over to Wandsworth to see his mother and collect his laptop. Gillian was alone when he got there, which gave him a bit of a guilt trip. He'd thought Brian was with her most of the time now.

"He's not here all the time."

"Oh, Mum, I'm sorry. Have you been left on your own a lot?"

"Not excessively, and in any case I quite enjoy it." There was a pause. "Charlie, be honest. What do you think of Brian?"

Charlie was caught on the back foot. "It's not up to me. What do you think of him?"

"He's good fun. I like his company, but it's getting a bit … overwhelming. If I want a drink, it's there almost before I can get up. When I sit down, he plumps up the cushions to make sure I'm comfortable."

"Maybe he just wants to look after you."

"No, it's more than that. It's like he wants me to be dependent on him."

"He's picked the wrong one there, hasn't he?"

"And there's another thing, though I hate to say it. I'm not altogether sure it's me he wants. I don't think he's in a particularly stable position financially. I'm beginning to wonder if it's my money he's after."

As Charlie had wondered the same thing, he found it difficult to respond. "You're a beautiful woman. Even I can see that. Look, this is your first fling since you had the sense at last to throw James out. You're free of commitments to anyone unless we need you, in which case believe me I'll come hollering for help, and I'm sure Kirsty would too. In the meantime, if it doesn't feel right, well, I'm sure you won't find it difficult to meet someone else. If you're still enjoying it, then carry on, but it's far too soon to be thinking of committing to another long-term relationship. Just concentrate on having a good time."

"Thank you, darling. You've put into words what I couldn't. It was quite nice to feel cherished, but my ankle's getting better and maybe it's time to assert myself. If Brian likes it, fine. If he doesn't, he can always leave. Now, how is Daisy?"

"Better, I think, but she still has a way to go. Do you mind if I see her through the weekend before I come back?"

"Of course not. Take as long as you like. As long as she needs. There's no point in adding to the difficulties by having to commute from here to walk the dogs and look after Daisy as well. If it's not too much for her, perhaps I'll drop in over the weekend. I'll phone and you can let me know."

The next day, Daisy squealed with delight when Charlie brought not just George and Mildred but also Muffin on what he called a flying visit.

"I checked with everyone that it was okay so they don't think they've been dognapped."

"Charlie, this is the best medicine you could have given me. Yes, I know. I love you too," she said to Muffin, who was licking her from chin to nose. They all sat on the sofa for a happy half hour until Charlie jumped up suddenly.

"What kind of a nurse am I? You haven't had lunch yet," he said.

"That's true, but neither have you."

"I'm not the invalid here. I'll rustle something up and you can eat it while I take this lot home. I'll have mine when I get back."

Cheese and biscuits and a pot of yoghurt appeared moments later, then Charlie left with the dogs. He was just closing the door of Muffin's home behind him when his phone rang. It was Jonathan.

"Hello, Jonathan. Calling to see how our patient is today?"

"I was wondering if I could come round for a little while. Maybe just for half an hour."

There was no justifiable reason to say no. "Could you just wait for a while, in case she's asleep?" Charlie hedged. "I'm out at the moment, but I'll be back soon to let you in."

Daisy was less than delighted by the prospect of a visit from her old boyfriend. She wanted to make the most of her time with Charlie, knowing full well that when she was better, he would be moving back to Wandsworth. However, when Jonathan arrived, she managed to appear warm and welcoming. Unfortunately, he took this as encouragement she hadn't intended. Charlie had tactfully removed himself and Daisy's suitor, sitting on the chair by the bed, grasped her hand and declared his undying love.

"I've missed you so much, Daisy. I don't know what went wrong before. Couldn't we try again? I'll be good to you, you know I will."

Daisy was flustered and didn't quite know how to handle the situation, a problem she wouldn't have had if she'd been fit and well. "No, Jonathan, don't. This isn't the time. I'm not well."

"I know, and I want to look after you."

"I'm being looked after. Please. Let's leave this for now."

Jonathan grasped at what he saw as an opening for the future. "You're right. Stupid of me. Put it down to the feelings of a man deeply in love."

Daisy couldn't believe what she was hearing. He'd never been one to give way to an excess of emotion. It was quite nice to see he was capable of it, though she wouldn't have wanted him to be distressed. They'd been through a lot in the two years they were together.

"Look, we'll talk about this when I'm better. Maybe go out for a meal or something."

She'd unintentionally given him hope, and with renewed good humour he shook Charlie's hand on the way out. Charlie wondered what he was looking so pleased about.

The rest of the day and the one that followed were fairly uneventful. Daisy became exhausted every time she had a shower or exerted herself in any way, but the recovery time was quicker. She was still sleeping a lot, but the waking periods were longer and spent now with Charlie rather than in bed. When the bell rang early on Friday evening, she was able to reassure her parents with a huge hug and a big smile.

"I see you haven't wasted any time. Have you unpacked yet?"

"No, kitten, we haven't even been home."

"You came straight round?"

"Of course we did, and we'd have come back sooner if we'd known how ill you were. You look really peaky. Charlie, you said she was okay."

"She was, Meirah, and I'm offended by the suggestion I haven't looked after her properly," Charlie joked, trying to make light of the situation. It was obvious by their reaction that both parents were shocked by Daisy's appearance. He'd become used to it over the past few days.

"I'm fine, Mum. I just get tired very quickly, and Charlie's been a fantastic nurse. A bit of a bully, really. Treats me like a naughty child."

"Best way to handle her, eh?" Mike asked Charlie.

"The only way."

Daisy wasn't sure she appreciated being discussed in this way. "Why don't we have a cup of tea? Then you can go home and settle in, and I'll be a good girl and go back to bed."

Meirah and Mike, satisfied that Daisy was in good hands, declined the invitation.

"Thank you, but no. Your mother and I have been driving for hours. We just wanted to make sure you were okay, which is still debatable, but I think we'll go home now. Is it okay if we come round tomorrow?"

"Of course it is, and it's Saturday so Charlie won't be walking the dogs. Maybe he can cook you lunch for a change?" She threw him a questioning glance, certain he wouldn't mind her offering his services.

"Yes, I've become quite proficient in the kitchen over the last few days. Tinned soup and yoghurt are my specialities, but I'll make an extra effort on your behalf. See you tomorrow, then, at say one o'clock."

"We'll look forward to it. Come on, Meirah, let's get you home. Bye, kitten."

After they'd left, Charlie raised an eyebrow at Daisy. "Fantastic nurse! And suggesting I cook lunch! I suppose having lived with Mike for most of your life, you take his culinary abilities for granted. How on earth am I going to compete?"

She thought for the minute that he was really worried, until she saw the twinkle in his eyes. "I'm sure you'll be able to rustle up something acceptable. After all, you haven't managed to kill me off yet and *I'm* not well."

CHAPTER FIFTEEN

Charlie was a competent cook and wanted to impress Daisy's parents. On Saturday, he restocked the kitchen and set about preparing lunch. When the doorbell rang, he assumed it was Mike and Meirah arriving early. He was surprised to see Gillian and Brian standing outside, having completely forgotten that his mother had said she'd come to visit over the weekend.

"Come in, come in. It's good to see you."

"Is it convenient? We didn't bother to phone, as we knew Daisy wouldn't be going anywhere for the time being, but if she's asleep we can…"

"No, it's fine." Charlie ran the menu through his mind and knew he'd made far too much for four people. "Can you stay for lunch? Mike and Meirah will be here in half an hour."

"We couldn't possibly intrude," Brian said politely.

"Of course we could. We don't stand on ceremony in our family. Thank you, Charlie, we'd love to."

When Meirah and Mike arrived, Charlie removed his laptop from the table and they were ready to go. Daisy, after a good morning's rest, was looking much better. At the table, Brian ate with his fork in one hand and his arm draped across the back of Gillian's chair. Her son could see exactly what she'd meant the other day and caught Mike looking at them rather sceptically. Obviously he didn't approve either.

They were having coffee when the doorbell rang again. *This should be fun*, Charlie thought as he ushered Jonathan into the room.

"You know Mike and Meirah, of course. This is my mother, Gillian, and Brian, a friend."

Jonathan looked acutely uncomfortable. He'd been hoping for a quiet time with Daisy to pursue his case.

"Nice to see you again, and to meet you," he said in that slightly pompous way he had.

"I'm afraid it's a bit of a fruitless visit," said Meirah. "Just look at Daisy. She's exhausted. Back to bed with you, young lady. Perhaps you could come back another time, Jonathan. Maybe call first to see if it's convenient."

In the face of such manipulation, there was little Jonathan could do but leave.

"I'll call you tomorrow, Daisy. Sleep well. Goodbye, everyone."

Nobody invited him to join the table and Charlie showed him out, filled with admiration for Meirah's masterly handling of the situation.

Daisy dutifully retired and the rest had a very enjoyable afternoon catching up on the past week. Nobody mentioned Jonathan.

"I'm getting fed up, Charlie," said Daisy the next day. "I'm sorry to complain, and I don't want you to think I'm not enjoying your company, but I'm beginning to feel like a prisoner here."

"A sure sign that you're getting better. Are you up for an outing? I could drive you to the park. I don't think you're fit enough to walk yet, but the fresh air might do you good."

"Oh, would you, Charlie?"

"Okay, finish your breakfast and we'll be off before you get too tired again."

A short while later they were standing in front of General Wolfe's statue facing the river, as they had once before with

Kirsty. It seemed so long ago now. They moved to one of the benches just as Charlie's phone rang.

"Hello, Jonathan. No, we're not at home. I've just driven Daisy to the park for a little break. Later? Hang on, I'll ask."

Daisy shook her head.

"Look, Jonathan, this is her first time out and it's tired her out. I think it will be back to bed for our invalid when we get home. Could you make it another time? Oh, that's a shame. Maybe next weekend then. Yes, call whenever you like."

He was rewarded with a smile from Daisy, who, let off the hook, could relax again.

"He's working all week. You have a reprieve, if that's what you want," said Charlie when he'd hung up.

"Thank you, Charlie. I just don't think I can cope with him at the moment."

"Understandable. He seems to agitate you rather than calm you down. Look, I know you were together for a long time. He seems pretty sincere about wanting you back, but I think you should wait until you're better before you make any decision. There, I've used my privilege as your brother to give my opinion. He's a nice guy, but at the moment you need to think about yourself rather than plunge back into a relationship."

"Thank you, Charlie. That's good advice," Daisy said in a very small voice. It seemed to her that he was promoting Jonathan's cause, just not at the moment. She'd been counting the days until Sam and Niall got back from their honeymoon. She desperately needed to talk to someone, and Sam was the only person she could possibly confide in. Thank goodness they were due back later that day. "I think you're right about going home, too. I am feeling tired."

Daisy did go to bed but only slept for about half an hour. That afternoon they sat together, she reading a book and he working on his laptop.

"It's leftovers tonight, if that's okay," said Charlie. "In spite of two extra people yesterday, there's still loads to eat."

"Suits me, and when I'm better perhaps I'll be able to cook something for you for a change."

"I shall look forward to it. Daisy, I was wondering, if the weather's nice again tomorrow, would you like me to come and collect you before I walk Muffin? You're not up to a whole morning, but a short walk might do you good."

It was agreed and Daisy was able to look forward to the next day with a lot more enthusiasm than she'd had for a while. As it turned out she was fine, and she realised that, one week after falling ill, she was probably almost back to normal. She had mixed feelings. Obviously she was delighted to be better, but didn't that herald Charlie's departure?

She phoned Sam the next morning while Charlie was out walking Oscar and the twins. "Was the trip everything you hoped for?" she asked.

"Daisy, I've never been so happy. All that misery seems so long ago now."

"I don't like to say I told you so, but I did."

"Are you all right? You sound a bit funny."

"I went to a wedding recently and was struck down with food poisoning."

"Oh, Daisy, no!"

"Of course not, but I have had a nasty strain of flu. I'm okay now. Look, Sam, I'd like to see you. I've got something I need to talk to you about. Can we do lunch one day this week?"

"I'll phone you later, Daisy. My boss, old grumpy-guts, is looking over his spectacles at me. Bye."

With that Daisy had to be content. She stood in the middle of the living room, looking round, trying to imagine what it would be like after Charlie left. She couldn't even remember what it had been like before. The phone rang. It was Meirah.

"How are you today, sweetheart?"

"I'm fine, Mummy. Much better."

"Would you like me to come round?"

"No. I really am much better. So much so that Charlie's coming back for me to walk Muffin."

"It'll do you good to get out again."

"Is Dad doing lunch tomorrow? Can we come, me and Charlie?"

"Of course you can. Take care then, and we'll see you tomorrow."

CHAPTER SIXTEEN

On Tuesday, Daisy and Charlie walked in the park together while Oscar was playing, Daisy now being well enough to do a whole morning. Spring was well and truly established now, and the fine weather had brought out more than the usual dog walkers. Gardeners were working on the flower borders, and the trees were festooned with blossom.

When they walked Oscar home, he no longer tugged on his lead. He recognised Charlie's authority and bowed to it.

"It's not fair. Do you know how long I've known this mutt?" Daisy scratched the top of Oscar's head. "You come along and charm him straight away."

"I wish I had the same success with women," Charlie said, trying to look crestfallen and failing. He decided it was time to bring up the idea he'd had. "I've been thinking, Daisy. What do you think about expanding the business?"

That stopped her in her tracks, all the more so when Oscar sat and waited patiently until they were ready to move again. "Look at him! You've got him eating out of your hand."

"Exactly my point. If this is work, bring it on. But you can't be making much out of it. In fact, I don't know how you manage."

"Barely, if you want the truth. I have to be very careful. I just can't imagine doing anything else."

"We could pool resources."

"Yeah! Your fortune and my piggy bank."

"I'm serious, Daisy. The tablets seem to be controlling my allergy, or maybe I'm just growing out of it. This should be the worst time of year for me here, but it seems to be only getting better. Whatever, I love what we do. Yes, we. There's no need for you to look at me like that. Whether you like it or not, we've been doing this together for weeks now, and since you've been ill I know I can do it as well as you can. I'd like to make it a permanent arrangement."

"And how do you propose doing that? You've already pointed out that there's very little money in it. It has to be a labour of love. What if you decide to go back to Australia?"

"Unlikely. Mum's staying here for the foreseeable future, and even if she doesn't I'm a big boy now. I love this country and I want to make it my home. What do you think, Daisy?"

"That still doesn't get round the fact that there's no money in it."

Charlie was quite excited now and did nothing to hide the fact. "We could buy a boarding kennel. Or build one. With a house attached, or maybe it's the other way round."

"But we'd have to give up Oscar and the rest. Property around here is far too expensive. We'd have to move further out."

"Look, without wanting to sound like I want to take over, I have more than enough money to set us up. I'm prepared to look upon it as a loss leader if the business will support itself after that. And like you, I couldn't bear the thought of not seeing Oscar, the twins and Muffin."

"You have given this a lot of thought, haven't you?"

"Yes, and I'd like you to as well. I've been online, researching the possibilities. I'm not pushing and there's no need for any false pride. You'd have to sell your flat, or maybe rent it out, and that would be your contribution."

"I hate to tell you, Charlie, but it isn't my flat. I'm housesitting for a friend. He's on a four-year course in America. I don't even pay rent. That's the reason I can keep my head above water. I'd have nothing to contribute financially at all."

"I'd prefer it if we were business partners, but if you're going to be precious about it you could always be an employee. That wouldn't be so different to what you do now."

"Why are you doing this, Charlie?"

"To annoy Kirsty, because she couldn't have a dog when we were at home," he said, smiling. "How can you ask, Daisy? I've found something here with you that I know will be fulfilling and rewarding, and which I believe would work commercially. And after this last week, we know we can live together in harmony, not that I've sampled too much of your cooking yet. But I know we could make a go of it. Don't give me an answer now. All I ask is that you think about it."

He'd almost held back because of Jonathan. If Daisy and he were to renew their relationship, the whole picture would change. There was no way he was prepared to share a home with Daisy *and* Jonathan. Somehow, though, walking with Daisy this morning, he hadn't been able to hold back any longer. A part of him knew he was being unfair by putting her in this position, particularly since in spite of her protestations of being well again she was still vulnerable.

"Of course I'll think about it, Charlie. It's a wonderful idea. It sounds almost too good to be true, but I don't want to feel like your pensioner. It isn't an equal partnership, not the way it stands. Anyway, obviously it would take some time to find the right premises, either custom-made or preferably a house with enough ground to build kennels alongside or behind, and then we'd have to get planning permission."

"Actually, I've already got my eye on one or two."

"One or two what?"

"Suitable properties. I've been looking, while you weren't well. I didn't have much else to do. I haven't been to see them in person yet. One's an existing business and the other would have to be started from scratch, but the possibilities are all there."

"Charlie!" she gasped.

"I was only looking!"

"That's what I used to say to Mum when we went shopping. She knew better, and so do I. And speaking of Mum, we'd better push on. We've still got the others to walk before we go to my parents' house for lunch."

"You see. You do have something to bring to the business. You'll be able to keep me focused."

In spite of promising Daisy he wouldn't say a word to her parents, the subject somehow got dropped into the conversation during lunch. Mike began to look thoughtful, but he brushed it aside when asked if something was on his mind.

"I expect you'll be going back to Wandsworth soon, now that Daisy's so much better," said Meirah.

This startled them both. Daisy felt her stomach turn over and she paled so quickly it was almost as if she was ill again. Charlie looked at Meirah and then at Daisy.

"You would think so, I suppose, but if Daisy and I are walking the dogs together every day, and if there's any chance this venture might get off the ground, it makes more sense for me to stay in Blackheath. If you'll have me, Daisy. I'll still do my share of the cooking."

"But it's only a one-bedroomed flat. You can't spend your life sleeping on a sofa bed."

"You're right, of course, but as a temporary measure, well, you said yourself it's a comfortable bed."

"And what about Gillian? She needs you now that Kirsty's gone."

"I don't think so. First of all, she only has the place on a six-month let, and secondly I believe she's enjoying her freedom. Brian's been good for her, but I don't think that will last."

He looked at Mike, who had steepled his fingers and was following the conversation with a good deal of interest. He had an ally there, he was sure.

"There will be others, though. She's an attractive and independent woman, and it's time she had a bit of fun. I'd only be inhibiting her if I lived in the same house."

"You seem to have covered so much already, Charlie. Have you asked her how she feels?" Mike asked.

"No, Mike. It wouldn't have been right until I'd discussed it with Daisy. I'm sorry I've burdened you with it. I wasn't supposed to say anything, it just slipped out."

Mike looked at him thoughtfully. "I like it. That's all I'm prepared to say at the moment, but I definitely like it."

Daisy met Sam for lunch the following day. Her friend was looking fantastic. Either marriage or pregnancy suited her, or both. She spent a while showing Daisy a few photos, some from the wedding and some from the honeymoon.

"Right, I've got forty-five minutes until I have to be back at work. What was it you wanted to talk about?" Sam asked.

Faced with the question, Daisy didn't know where to start. Finally she said, "Charlie."

"Charlie? What about him?"

"Ever since I stumbled into his arms on the doorstep the day I met him, I've been having inappropriate feelings."

"Oh, Daisy, no!"

"Oh, Sam, yes. I've got so much to tell you and I don't know what to do."

"How does he feel about you? Do you know?"

"I'm his sister. That's how he treats me, and I wouldn't expect anything else." She paused and tried to gather her thoughts. "He stayed with me last week, while you were away and I was ill."

"But you've only got one bedroom."

"Sofa bed. It was wonderful, Sam. We get on so well. Even in my misery I was happy not to be well so I could have him with me."

"And he's going back to Gillian now?"

"No. At least, I'm not sure." The whole story came tumbling out.

"And Jonathan's turned up again! Deep joy."

"Yes, I know." Daisy looked a bit sheepish. "For a while there I was actually considering it. If I can't have Charlie, at least I could be comfortable with Jonathan."

"Comfortable and bored out of your mind. Whatever were you thinking of? For goodness' sake, turn the poor man loose."

"You're right, I know you are. I feel really bad about it, but I honestly wasn't feeling well enough to deal with him as well as everything else. I'm sure Charlie thinks I want him back."

"Do you think it's wise, Daisy, going into business with him? Living in the same house on a permanent basis?"

"No, definitely not wise."

"But you're going ahead with it."

"I'm thinking about it. Now that Kirsty's gone back to Australia, I only have a brother."

"Which would be fine if that was the way you were thinking about him, but you're not."

"You've always been straight with me, Sam. Tell me what to do."

"I can't, Daisy. You know I can't. If it was only about your feelings for him, it would be easy. I'd tell you to cut and run, because frankly I can only see you ending up hurt. What if he meets someone and wants her to move in with him?"

Daisy's blood ran cold.

"But it isn't as simple as that," Sam went on. "He's offering you your dream on a plate. It's what you've always wanted, ever since you were a teenager. Almost impossible to turn down, I'd say. The trouble is, you can't even try it on for size. It's not like an ordinary job. If you agree, you're in it for the whole ride."

"I wonder what properties he has in mind. I didn't think to ask him."

"You see, you're not even really listening to me. I think you have to give it a go. I also think you have to be prepared to have your heart broken."

"It's probably already too late for that. The first thing I have to do, though, is tell Jonathan we don't have a future together. Would it be awful if I did it on the phone?"

"Actually, I don't think so. If he waits until the weekend to come round, you're only keeping his hopes alive. It wouldn't be a nice way to do it if you were already going out with him, but you're not. It's probably kinder if you just tell him next time he calls. At least then your mind will be free to deal with this other problem."

"And my heart, Sam? That's never going to be free again. I've heard of cousins getting together before, but a half-brother and sister! It's unnatural. The trouble is, Sam, it doesn't feel unnatural."

"Come and look at this, Daisy," Charlie said when she got home. "Tell me what you think."

He patted the place beside him on the sofa and showed her the webpage he was looking at. She recognised the place immediately. A boarding kennel in her own area — of course she knew it. She'd never been inside, though, having had no pretext and not liking to ask if she could have a look around. The living accommodation was all on the first floor, the ground being given over to a grooming parlour and small examination room for those minor ailments that could be dealt with onsite. Apart from that, there were washing facilities for the dogs and a boot room which also housed lockers. Another room was laid out with six kennels with individual runs, presumably for dogs whose owners didn't want them to be housed outside. Lastly, there was a huge room given over to feeding preparations.

"Ready?" Charlie asked and scrolled down to show Daisy the back of the property. Additional kennels were ranged down either side of what should have been the garden, each with its own run. It looked like a perfect set-up. Daisy turned to him with saucer-like eyes.

"Charlie, it's amazing! How long has it been on the market? How much do they want for it?" She blanched when he showed her the price. "Do you really have that sort of money?"

Charlie smiled. "Actually, I do. Should I apologise?"

"Of course not. I'm just not used to talking in those figures. This is too one-sided, Charlie. I can't offer anything by comparison."

"But you can, Daisy. In fact, I couldn't do it without you. I don't know anything about feeding and grooming, and a place this size needs someone to manage it. You've had the training. I don't want to employ someone from the outside."

"We'd need staff. There's no way two of us could run a venture on this scale."

"It doesn't say how many dogs they have on a regular basis, and some of the business must be seasonal. Perhaps extra hands are needed during the summer and Christmas holidays, a good opportunity for students, maybe. They mention a local vet as well. Is it one you know?"

"Yes. They have a good reputation."

"Okay, let's have a look at the other place." He pulled up a picture that showed a house in need of fixing up. "It's much cheaper."

"Cheaper, but hardly cheap," she interrupted.

"But with a lot of potential. We'd have to get planning permission for this one, and I can see it taking a few months to get it in working order."

"And I can see the appeal, but ultimately would it be any cheaper than the other one? If there isn't much difference in cost, why take on such a huge project?"

He smiled.

"You like a project. I see," said Daisy with a laugh. "Well, it looks like we're having our first disagreement. It makes more sense to me to buy an established business. If you can see the accounts and the figures add up, why would you speculate on something else?"

"You see. I do need you as a business partner, not just a manager. What do you think?"

"Give me time, Charlie. This is all very new to me. I don't know how long you've been thinking about it, but it's going to take me a while to get used to the idea."

"Okay. I promise not to push." He paused. "Do you fancy a drive? We could have a look at the outside."

Daisy burst out laughing. "Come on, then. It won't hurt to have a look."

When Daisy saw the place, she found herself being drawn in. It was amazing from the outside, and she knew from the photos that the inside was pretty impressive as well. Charlie took her out to dinner that evening, to celebrate the fact that they might be celebrating, he'd said. She had little resistance. Part of the dream was better than none at all.

With her phone on silent in the restaurant, Daisy missed Jonathan's call. She was glad he hadn't been able to get through. It would have spoiled her evening. It was late when they got home, so she sent a text saying she was sorry and would call tomorrow, but he rang back immediately. As it turned out, he took the news fairly well.

"I think I already knew. I just want to say that you can call me any time, no strings attached. Be happy, Daisy."

It was that quick and easy, but there was a tinge of sadness too. Charlie had been in the kitchen making coffee, unaware she'd been on the phone. She didn't tell him.

CHAPTER SEVENTEEN

On Saturday afternoon, Daisy and Charlie were invited to Meirah and Mike's house. They were delighted to see Daisy looking so much better. Meirah, with the inevitable splashes of paint dotted about her person, ushered them into the studio for opinions on her latest creation.

"Have you had the Daisy portrait framed yet, Charlie? I'd like to see it if I may," she said.

"And you shall, but I'm waiting until I find a permanent home."

"We've never shown you the whole place, have we, Charlie?" Mike butted in. "Fancy a look around?"

Charlie accepted with enthusiasm, excited to explore a home as large and apparently rambling as this one. "We've got some wonderful Victorian properties back home and some of the old colonial stuff is amazing, but I've never seen anything in this style. It's fantastic."

"Yes, we fell for it as soon as we saw it. Come on. I'll show you outside."

The property had once been a smallholding, and though they didn't keep any farm stock Charlie was delighted to see a flourishing vegetable patch and knew he'd sampled some of its produce. There were a couple of horses in one of the paddocks.

"It's let out at the moment. We weren't doing anything with it, and it's nice to have some animals around, even if they aren't ours. Keeps the grass down too."

"Is that yours too?" Charlie asked, looking at a bungalow built in the style of the main house.

"Yes, the previous owners had it built as a holiday cottage for a secondary income, but we've never pursued that option. We tried to persuade Daisy to take it when she moved out, but she wanted to be closer to town and she had this free rental offer from her friend Angus. She said she wasn't confident about building up a customer base here. It's much more rural and spread out than Blackheath. She had her regulars, of course, like she does now, but I think she just wanted to break away. It was time."

"Why have you never rented it out, if you don't mind me asking? It's far away enough from the main house not to disturb you, I'd have thought."

"The simple answer is we were lucky enough not to need to. I did think at one time Meirah might have used it as a studio, but she's happier in the house. Do you want to see inside?"

It might have come straight out of the pages of a magazine. Decorated and equipped with immaculate taste, one bedroom was set up as a double and the other as a twin. The lounge had a wood-burning stove with a dining area at one end that easily accommodated the sizeable table that was there. The kitchen had a range and was large enough to house an island in the centre. The units had been fitted a long time ago and could have done with updating, but that was just a matter of taste.

"I've been tempted once or twice to cook here. It seems a shame for that range to go to waste, but it's too far from the house."

"Do you ever have friends to stay?"

"Oh, yes. The people we went to visit last week have been here a few times. They always stay in the house with us, though."

Mike took Charlie back outside, where he could see the two paddocks as well as the garden, all of which sloped gently down to a small stream which Mike told him was their boundary.

"The outbuilding down there is where Meirah keeps an easel and some equipment. If I can't find her on a lovely summer day, I know exactly where to look. Shall we join the girls now?"

Daisy and Meirah had laid the table for tea in the kitchen, the hub of this huge home. Once Meirah was satisfied that her daughter had made a full recovery, she stopped sending her guarded glances.

"Sit down, everyone," she said when Mike and Charlie had returned. "Time for tea."

"I thought we were coming for dinner," said Charlie. "Oh, I'm sorry. That must have sounded so rude."

"No, Charlie, it didn't, and you were right."

"It's just that, in the face of homemade scones and farmhouse cakes, how on earth are we going to be able to tackle one of Mike's famous dinners later?"

"We thought we might all go for a walk, show you the village and surrounding area. That way, we can work off tea and build up an appetite for later."

"There's no arguing with that, Meirah. I love being given an excuse to indulge myself."

It was still quite warm when they set off an hour later into the lovely Kent countryside. Charlie spotted a windmill on a nearby hill, while Daisy squealed delightedly at the sight of lambs playing in one of the fields.

"Anything with four legs and she goes to mush," her father commented to Charlie. They were following Meirah and Daisy along the lane, hugging the hedge at the infrequent passing of a vehicle.

"You may have realised I had an ulterior motive for bringing you out here today."

Charlie hadn't and said so.

"I don't usually give people a guided tour, but I've been thinking about what you said on Tuesday about the kennels."

Charlie stopped in his tracks.

"No, keep moving. I don't want Daisy to know what we're discussing. I'm going to talk for a bit and I want you to listen. You can ask questions later. I like the way you're ready to take on something completely new simply because it's what you want to do. It's obvious you take after your mother. I think she must have had a challenge or two in her time, from some of the things she's told Meirah. Anyway, you got me thinking. You can see I've got a whole parcel of land here that's virtually standing idle. I took the liberty of taking a look at the two properties you're interested in in Blackheath. I can see the appeal of both, though I'd go for the up and running business. I can also understand that the challenge of starting from scratch has a certain appeal for you.

"My daughter has a mind of her own, a little stubborn streak. You need a good argument that makes sense to her. I'm sure you're beginning to follow my drift now. I'd be willing to give you the bungalow and the land you need if you finance and organise the building of the kennels. It'll be far more even-handed that way and, as such, more acceptable to Daisy."

"If she's so independent that she moved out, what makes you think she'd be any more willing to accept such a gift from you?" Charlie asked.

"Practicalities, mostly. That and the fact that children are usually more ready to take things from their parents."

"I don't know what to say, Mike. There's so much to consider here. It's a beautiful setting, no doubt about it, and I'd love it out here. I'm not sure how Daisy would feel about moving further away from town."

"Nor am I. It's only a twenty-minute journey on a good run, but if you're trying to get into Blackheath during the morning rush hour, that's another thing entirely. I bring it up because I don't think there's anything that would prise her away from Oscar and the rest. If we do go ahead, you'd both have to live here. It wouldn't be practical otherwise, so one of you is going to have to do the commute while the other remains behind, or you could alternate. It would completely alter the nature of your walks, but that would probably happen anyway, even if you bought in Blackheath. Are you with me so far?"

"I am, and I've got a few questions."

"Hang on until I'm finished. For a start, we don't even know if we can get planning permission, and that's the real reason I don't want to discuss it with Daisy yet. I've spoken to a friend, a local councillor, who tells me there is no other similar venture in the immediate vicinity and he can't see why there would be an objection. We're not close enough to the nearest property to worry about noise impacting any neighbours, and it's not like we're wanting to build a factory."

"No, that would be criminal in a place like this."

"I've another reason, Charlie, for making this proposal. I'm not working full-time anymore and I'm not too keen on my commute either, though I'm happy to say I don't have to join the throng that makes its way into London every day. I've been thinking for some time of signing things over to my partner. We've been talking about it since before you arrived in England. He's willing to buy me out. He's got a son waiting in the wings for promotion. I wouldn't want to be idle, though, and that brings me to the next point. I could help and it would give me an interest on my doorstep. I don't think Meirah would appreciate it if I kept interrupting her painting because I wanted company. So, ask any questions you have and then go away and think about it."

"I don't know what to say. You seem to have answered most of them already. Obviously we'd have to get plans drawn up and approved in outline before we can do anything else. If there's a barrier there, we can't even get off the ground."

"I'll leave you to get the plans done. I can recommend an architect if you like. Then we'll see what the Council says. Time enough then for you to make a decision and definitely time enough to tell Daisy."

"You seem very determined to keep it from her."

Mike smiled. "Yes, for two reasons. Firstly, I don't want her to set herself against it before we have a firm plan to put in front of her and secondly…" He paused. "Secondly, I'd love to have her close to home, and I'm terrified she'll say no."

"Do you fancy a coffee before we turn in?" asked Charlie once he and Daisy had returned to Blackheath.

"I'm really tired, Charlie, but yes please, that would be lovely."

They settled on the sofa with their mugs.

"Happy thoughts?" said Charlie,

"Happy, excited, but still to be convinced."

"Which is what I don't want to do. You have to find your way through this yourself, Daisy. There's nothing I'd like more, but we're coming from different places here. I've always wanted to find something to invest my time in. I never expected my heart to go there too. You, on the other hand, already have your time and heart invested in your current work."

"Don't misunderstand me, Charlie. I'm keen on the venture — I just don't know which property we'll go for. We both know I don't have any money, but I can contribute experience you have yet to gain. I'm willing to give it a try as long as you put me on a salary and let me do my job. But it has to be done legally."

"Of course."

"And we'll need to thrash out the details of my contract."

"Again, of course."

"Okay, which is it to be then? The going concern or the falling-to-pieces project?"

"Give me a few days, Daisy. I need to work out details and…" He paused. "There may be another option."

With that she had to be content. He wouldn't budge.

"Let's sleep on it. On Monday I'll have to get to work, and I'll be busy with facts and figures in the morning. Before it gets to the stage where our lives are no longer our own, and it surely will, how about you show me some more of your beautiful city tomorrow afternoon?"

CHAPTER EIGHTEEN

Gillian met them outside St Paul's Cathedral the next day. They climbed the 259 steps to the Whispering Gallery.

"Just be careful, Charlie. Anything you say can be heard on the other side," said Daisy.

"You're kidding me!"

"Would I lie to you?"

Daisy and Gillian decided this was exercise enough though Daisy was well and truly better and Gillian's ankle wasn't showing any signs of discomfort.

"Best not to push it, though," said Gillian. "I've had enough massages to last me a lifetime."

Charlie insisted they wait while he made his way to the Golden Gallery at the top.

Daisy had picked up on Gillian's comment and raised an eyebrow. "Brian?"

"Sadly no longer."

"He's dead?" Daisy gasped.

"No, it's not as bad as that. I just don't think I was cut out to be the cherished little woman. It was suffocating. You know what they say, Daisy. It was good while it lasted."

"Well, I'm glad, if that's what you really want."

"It's been an edifying experience, but I'm ready to move on now. Here comes Charlie, looking very pleased with himself."

"That was brilliant! Are you sure you don't want to go up?"

"Next time. Meanwhile, I was just telling Daisy that I've finished with Brian. Isn't that an awful expression? Like he was something to be picked up and discarded. Never mind. I don't think he'll lose any sleep over it. I certainly shan't. Shall we go and have one of those splendid cream teas to celebrate?"

"I don't need asking twice. Is it okay if I bring your car back tomorrow afternoon? Now that Daisy's well enough to drive again, we can use hers."

"Oh, can we?" said Daisy, raising her eyebrows.

"And you'll be wanting it if you haven't got Brian hanging around your shoulders anymore," Charlie went on.

"Actually, I'm thinking of taking a short trip to Edinburgh," said Gillian. "Apparently there might be some family there from way back. I'll try and track them down, but if I can't it doesn't matter. I want to go anyway. I can fly up from City Airport, and maybe I'll do a coach tour as well. If I do go, it'll be in the next week or two, so you're welcome to keep the car for the time being. I can get taxis in the meantime."

"Thank you, then I will. I'll be running around in the next few days, so it would be useful, in case Daisy wants to use her car."

"Can we talk about this?" Daisy interrupted. "My car still isn't insured for you to drive."

"No, but that's easily arranged."

"You're pushing, Charlie."

Charlie looked at her, contrition spreading across his face. "You're right," he said. "I'm sorry — I was getting carried away. This is never going to work if you think I'm trying to tell you what to do. If it happens again, just pull me up."

"You can be sure of that."

"Okay, you two, what's going on here?"

"Mum, Daisy and I are thinking of going into business together."

Gillian was delighted when they explained the scheme, incomplete though it was. "I didn't think you'd be able to sit still for very long. You always did like getting your hands dirty. Looks like you'll be doing it for real this time."

"Oh no, Mum, Daisy's going to be doing the mucky stuff. I'll be dealing with the organisation and admin."

Daisy almost rose to the bait.

"What about your travel plans?"

Gillian's question startled Daisy. She had forgotten about Charlie's plans to see the world.

"A man can't do everything, Mum. You know what I'm like — I have to do this now," said Charlie. "In any case, if we decide to go with the purchase of the existing business, we'll have to register our interest quickly. The derelict property won't hang around forever either."

"It's derelict!"

"A slight exaggeration. I've got something else in mind as well."

A sideways glance from Daisy told him she'd quite like to know what the something else was. "Charlie, if we're going to work together, I have to have the full picture, not just the snippets you choose to share with me."

"She's quite right," Gillian agreed.

"I know, and I promise to be completely straight with you, Daisy, but I need a few days to see if it's viable. You may be disappointed with this other proposal or you may not, but if it won't get off the ground I don't want it to discourage you."

"You're talking in riddles."

"Give me a few days. The end of the week should do it. Then I'll tell you everything and the decision will be yours."

"But that's not right either. Whatever it is, it needs to be a joint decision."

"There's no pleasing you sometimes."

"No, but she's right again, Charlie. If this is going to be a partnership, it needs to be equal, if not financially then certainly from every other point of view."

Charlie threw his hands up in defeat. "Two of you at once. I've got no chance. Look, Daisy, please just give me until Friday. After that, I promise I'll never have any secrets from you ever again."

Throughout the following week, the coffee table was strewn with Charlie's sketches and notes, and he was constantly on his laptop. He spent a lot of time on the phone as well, keeping Mike up to date. He also spoke to someone on the Council and even went to see him with some sketches one morning while Daisy was out. His advice had been to prepare detailed plans and submit them in the usual way, at the same time reassuring Charlie that he could see no reason why permission shouldn't be granted. Charlie and Mike decided they would tell Daisy at the next Tuesday lunch. Depending on her answer, they would proceed or go to plan B, the established business.

"You promised you'd tell me on Friday."

"I did, and I will if you insist, but there's a reason I want to wait until we see your parents. It's up to you."

"I don't suppose another three days will make that much difference."

"Daisy, will you be sorry to leave this flat?"

"In a way. I love the position, but I've been here for nearly four years now, and I'd have to leave anyway after Angus comes home. Maybe it's time to move on. I would have to keep a close check on the flat, though, if we go before he gets back. I promised. Why do you ask now of all times?"

"Because I've loved the time we've had here. Even in such close proximity, we haven't got on each other's nerves. It's just that I'd like a room of my own and somewhere Mum, and maybe even Kirsty and Cam, can come and stay when they want to."

"I can appreciate that."

"Look, I'm not putting this very well. I just want to be sure you're ready to throw in a way of life you love for another. I'd hate to think I'd pushed you into something you don't want to do."

Daisy put her head on one side and pulled at one of her curls. She was smiling. "You think you could?"

"I honestly don't know. I get a bit carried away, and sometimes I sweep people along with me."

He was sitting on the sofa. Standing in front of him, she put her hands on his shoulders and looked him straight in the eye.

"Charlie, you have presented me with the possibility of my dream becoming a reality. There's no pushing here from either of us. Our goal is the same. I'm just as excited about it as you are. Possibly even a teensy bit more."

Her face was so close to his he had no idea how he managed not to kiss her. Instead, he grabbed her in a bear hug. It would have to do.

The grey week gave way to sunshine, and by the time they set off for Kent on Tuesday both were looking forward to the promised barbecue. Daisy was bubbling over with excitement. Today would be the day Charlie would reveal his plans and she'd know what her future was to hold.

When the proposal was laid out after lunch, it left her open-mouthed.

"And you knew? You all knew!" she exclaimed. "Don't mind me. It's only my life you're talking about."

It took the combined efforts of her parents and Charlie to calm her down and explain why they hadn't told her.

"Charlie needed to find out what the chances were of the proposal being accepted. How would you have felt if you'd really fallen for the idea and then somebody said we couldn't go ahead?"

"I'd have felt like a grown-up, Dad, which is not how you've all treated me."

"We were trying to protect you, Daisy."

"You too, Mum? I thought it was only the men who thought I was a wilting flower."

"Not that, of course, but you have been quite ill. We were just trying to look after you." Meirah stroked her daughter's hair, much as she had done when Daisy was a child. "These two will probably use every argument they have to try to persuade you to take up the offer, and their arguments are good ones. All I will say is that you'll make your parents very happy if you decide to come back home. The bungalow will be yours and we won't interfere, but it would be nice to have you close at hand."

Daisy gripped her mother's hands, holding her gaze steady.

"Don't even think about giving an answer now," Meirah went on. "This is much too big a thing for a quick decision."

There were noises of protest from Charlie and Mike.

"No, you two. Leave her alone. Give the girl some credit. She has to do what she feels is best for her. There are lots of things to consider, not the least of which is whether or not she wants to work with her father. Great for me, of course. It'll keep you out of my hair."

"Unlike that delightful shade of blue which is adorning your already lovely curls," Mike teased.

Meirah smiled at her husband. "Come on, Daisy. Walk down to the stream with me. We'll leave the men to drown their frustrations in a glass of beer."

Daisy spent a sleepless night worrying what to do for the best. Mystery property number three. Home. It appealed, no doubt about that, and it made sense. Almost four years had passed since she'd lived with her parents. The bungalow was far enough away from the house that her comings and goings would not easily be observed, unless they were actually watching from the window. She gave them more credit than to think they would do that.

She wasn't a teenager anymore, but she did sometimes come home very late after a night out with friends. Would the sound of her car on the gravel drive disturb them? And what of her friends, most of whom lived in the Blackheath vicinity? Might she be cutting herself off from them? None of these were insurmountable problems. Once she was in the car, it was immaterial whether or not she added an extra half an hour to her journey. What really gave her pause was the logistical problem of walking Oscar and the rest. Turning onto her side, she decided that this must be the most important consideration and she would discuss it with Charlie in the morning.

"Did you sleep well?" Charlie asked Daisy the next day.

"Not really," she replied. "Far too much to think about. You?"

"No. I kept thinking how difficult it must have been for you having this curved ball thrown into the equation. Your mother was right — it isn't a decision to be taken lightly. I'm sorry if you thought I was rushing you. I *was* rushing you. I just didn't realise."

"In all fairness, though I'm still a bit resentful about being excluded, I think I would have been the world's worst person to live with if I'd known what was going on. We need to talk, Charlie."

"Of course we do. Do you want to start?"

"Let's try to be practical here. You may think I'm being silly, but I can't do anything without considering the impact on Oscar and the others. So let's make them the priority and work around that."

"I understand — they have a place in my heart that would be difficult to fill. Is that what's holding you back from Home Farm? If it is, we have to decide if it's viable for us to take it in turns to come back and walk them. And it would mean taking turns, because I'm no more prepared to leave them than you are."

"So what do you think?"

"Economically it's a no-no. By the time you take into account the petrol and the hours spent when we could both be working, it makes no sense at all. The business will take all our time, I'm sure, both during the setting-up process and eventually the running. However, your father would be an extra pair of hands we wouldn't have if we settled in Blackheath. That would account for the difference in cost, bearing in mind we wouldn't have to employ anyone as we almost certainly would here. Emotionally there's no argument, which leaves us with the question, are we prepared to commute, and does the idea of living back in Kent appeal to you?"

"I'm quite surprised, but actually it does."

"So we go ahead?"

"I think so, yes."

CHAPTER NINETEEN

Charlie phoned his sister later that day.

"Kirsty, Daisy and I wanted you to know we're going into business together."

"All this leisure not suiting you then?"

"It was okay for a while, but you know me. I need to have a project."

"So, what's it to be then?"

"Are you sitting down?"

"No, but I will if you think it necessary."

"It might be."

"Okay, I'm sat."

Charlie told her, smiling as he did because he was pretty sure he knew what her response would be. He wasn't disappointed.

"You are kidding me!"

"No."

"Charlie, you don't know how lucky you are to be thousands of miles away! I can't believe it. Dogs! After all these years of being allergic to them."

"The medication seems to be working," he said meekly.

Kirsty made an indecipherable spluttering sound.

"How's Cam?"

"Don't you dare try to change the subject!"

"Well, I'm happy to talk about it all day, but I didn't think you would be."

"You bet your life I'm not. You might as well tell me, though. Any concrete plans, other than the large piece I'm aiming to drop on your head the next time I see you?"

Charlie outlined the venture and brought Kirsty up to date with Gillian's news before they said goodbye.

"What did she say?" Daisy asked, coming into the room just as the call finished.

"Only that she wants to drop a concrete slab on my head."

"Hmm. I feel like that too sometimes."

The next few weeks were rewarding and frustrating in equal measure. They were able to obtain outline planning consent fairly quickly, but progress after that was slow.

Gillian returned from Scotland, where she'd had a wonderful time, staying an extra week and declaring an affinity with the country that she'd never felt anywhere else. The missing relatives were nowhere to be found, in spite of visits to the records office and the area from which she thought they'd come. Daisy wondered how she felt, remembering her own emotions when discovering family she never knew she had.

"It would have been nice, of course, but I have my children and my brother, who is there even though we rarely communicate. Then there's you and your parents. It would be impossible to tell you, Daisy, how I feel about you. I honestly regard you as another daughter and as for your mother, who could not love her? Mike is just an all-round nice guy. I feel as if I've been given a new life in so many ways."

Gillian was showing a sentimental side that was nothing like the face she normally presented to the world. Daisy thought she was learning to drop her guard now that James was gone. He must have been hell to live with.

"Are you happy about the project, Gillian? I don't suppose it's anything like what you imagined Charlie would end up doing."

"I couldn't be more pleased. He was ready to move on. The sale of the business back home was as much for him as for me. He'd gone as far with it as he could. This will be more than a business. It will be a lifestyle and it will suit him. Even Kirsty's pleased. The teasing about dogs and allergies are just that, teasing."

Summer flew by and life settled into a comfortable if temporary pattern. Daisy continued the daily walks and for the most part Charlie went with her, though there were times when he had appointments with architects and planners that kept him away.

"It isn't the same when he's not there," Daisy told Sam one day when they met for lunch.

"Nor will it ever be if you're going to have to split the walks when you move to Kent. Are you sure you can cope with all this? Nothing's signed yet. There's still time to back out."

Daisy looked at Sam as if she was speaking a foreign language. "I thought you of all people would understand, Sam. This is my dream."

"But Charlie has become your dream too, and one that can never become a reality. Are you really prepared to spend your life living with the man you love, one who obviously holds you in deep but platonic affection?"

"I have to, Sam."

"But you don't, Daisy. You can go back to the way things were. Stay in your flat. Walk Oscar and the rest."

"Angus?"

"Another flat then."

"There is no going back. If I pull out, if I try to resume my life as it was before, it just wouldn't work for me. Every day would be a reminder. I'd have to do something completely different to survive, and that would mean saying goodbye to the dogs. No, Sam, I'm going through with it."

It was good that Daisy had Sam as an outlet. The constant rein she was having to put on her emotions was wearing to say the least.

"How are my godchildren doing?" she asked, changing the subject and lightening the mood in a flash.

The smile on Sam's face told her everything she needed to know. "Fighting with each other already, I'm sure, judging by the amount they're moving around. And they're not even born yet! I can't imagine what it'll be like in a few years."

"Probably just as well you can't. If you're lucky, you'll get some peace between the terrible twos and the terrible teens."

As they stood to leave, Sam asked, "Daisy, does my bum look big in this?"

"I'm in no position to comment, as it's impossible to see where your bum ends and your tum begins."

They left the café, giggling like a couple of schoolgirls. Daisy walked Sam to her office. She still had several weeks before beginning maternity leave.

"How's Niall?"

"Grumpy this morning, because he was being kicked in the back all night."

"Still can't control your temper, eh?"

"Very amusing. I didn't mention that it would be worse after the twins arrive. That's when the fun will really start."

"Are Aileen and Fergal planning on coming over?"

"They can't wait. Fortunately Mammy can come at the drop of a hat."

"Mammy?"

"Aileen asked if I'd call her Mammy. It's lovely, isn't it? If Fergal's held up by work, he'll follow when he can. It depends on whether or not I'm on time. The run up to Christmas is a busy period for him, and the twins are due in the middle of November."

Apart from the calls that were made when she and Charlie were together, Daisy and Kirsty skyped or facetimed every week.

"How's Cam?" asked Daisy during one of their chats.

"Busy and leaving most of the wedding arrangements to me. I've talked to Mum about it, same as with you, and sent several links showing the sort of thing I want. The venue's booked, the caterers arranged and the menu is up for discussion. Mum's promised to come home in January for a while. Hopefully there'll be plenty of time then, if the dress needs to be fitted, for it to be ready by the beginning of April."

"Two weddings twelve months apart and two babies in between. It will have been an eventful year by the time you take your vows."

"No gorgeous bloke on your horizon yet, Daisy?"

"Nor likely to be. I guess I was destined to be an aunt or a godmother. And I have my dogs. Well, other people's dogs, but you know what I mean. There's obviously no hope for me"

Daisy was flippant but she'd decided very firmly that second-best wasn't good enough. If she couldn't have the man she wanted, then marriage wasn't for her. The experience with Jonathan had taught her that if nothing else.

"There's always hope."

If only she knew. The one thing she found difficult with Kirsty was that she couldn't talk openly about their brother.

"Have you heard from James?" Daisy asked.

"Not a word. I'm not even sure if he knows I've flown home. Or if he cares."

"Do you find that hard? He brought you up, after all."

"I'd hardly call it that, Daisy. He was there, I give you that, but as far as bringing me up, no, that was entirely Mum's domain. He didn't even read me a bedtime story, not that I can remember, anyway."

"Will he be at the wedding?"

"No way. I can't forgive the way he treated Mum all those years. She deserved better. It wasn't for me to say anything while they were together, but he was done a long time ago as far as I'm concerned."

Later that week, a letter from the council arrived.

"They've turned us down!" Charlie exclaimed, reading it quickly. "I can't believe it."

"Oh, Charlie, no," Daisy wailed. "What does it say? What's gone wrong?"

"Wait a minute, let me see." She was on tenterhooks while he had another look. She saw him relax. "Right. It's not as bad as I thought. They just want a couple of fairly minor amendments. If we comply with those, they'll turn it round by the end of the week," he said, beaming at her.

"Oh my God! Does that mean we can start soon? How long will it take? Will we be up and running by Christmas?"

"Hardly, I'd have thought. Look at all the foundation work that has to be done first before any building work begins. It might be best, though, if we consider moving ourselves as soon as it starts. There are some mistakes that can be remedied easily, but there are others that might involve our input. What do you think, Daisy? Are you ready?"

Daisy took a deep breath and looked around her, at the flat that had been her home for four years now. In a way she'd be sad to leave, but something potentially great was pulling her away. She'd spoken to Angus in America, letting him know she might have to go sooner than they'd planned. He'd been very supportive and had told her that he'd offer the flat to his brother.

"Ready when you are," said Daisy. "Don't you think we ought to tell Mum and Dad the news first?"

"Yes, but I also think I need to sit down with these plans, make the amendments, and get them copied and couriered over. We're not there yet, Daisy."

CHAPTER TWENTY

Meirah and Mike were delighted, and when the anticipated permission came through a few days later Daisy and Charlie moved to the bungalow at Home Farm. They arrived on Friday afternoon, she in her car and he in the small van they'd hired to move their few belongings. The flat had come furnished, pleasantly so, but its contents were not theirs to take. At the bungalow, they found the fridge filled, the beds made and three different vases of flowers waiting for them.

"Go and settle in, but we're expecting you for dinner this evening. Before you protest, we will not put upon you or presume you will eat with us every day. Tonight, though, is a celebration," said Meirah.

"And just so that you know, I've made arrangements with my partner and I'll be officially retired from the company at the end of the month," added Mike.

Charlie at last framed and hung Meirah's painting of Daisy, and they invited Meirah to come and see it.

She gasped when she went into the lounge. "Charlie, it's perfect!"

"I'm so glad you're pleased with it," he said. "I'd have hated for you to be disappointed."

Meirah's artistic temperament showed itself in a display of emotion. Charlie received a huge hug. It wasn't often she got to see her work displayed, other than at an exhibition. Those she sold went to their new homes and disappeared from her life forever, though she kept a photo album of all her paintings.

"I'll be reminded of Daisy at that age every time I come. She was a pretty child, wasn't she?"

Nobody argued with her. Daisy just looked embarrassed.

Work was due to begin on Monday morning, and as the weather was being kind they spent Sunday in the country. Mike drove them to some of his favourite beauty spots, places Charlie had never seen. The pub lunch was more than acceptable, and they came home ready to face the onslaught the next morning, each in their own way aware that things would never be the same again.

The main house faced the lane, and access to the bungalow was via a long, wide drive on the right-hand side. The smaller building stood well back and at right angles, giving privacy to both dwellings. A little further up the lane past Home Farm Cottage was the field that was to house the kennels. A new drive would be laid here, separating the business from the accommodation. Services would be run to the site, foundations dug, and so would begin a time of organised chaos. When all was complete, the bungalow would have a line of sight to the kennels, whereas the house, with no window on that side, would be screened completely.

It was with some reluctance that Daisy drove off on Monday morning, leaving Charlie to supervise the arrival of the first workers. She had an uneventful journey, but she knew something was wrong as soon as she turned into the road. The smell of smoke assailed her nostrils. As she parked outside Oscar's home, she was horrified to find that it was a burnt-out shell. Leaping out of the car, she rushed over to where a small number of people were standing outside the tape barrier that had been set up.

"What happened?" Daisy almost screamed at one of the neighbours whom she recognised.

"They're not sure yet. The whole place went up in flames on Saturday night."

"What about the people inside?"

"From what I understand, they're lucky to be alive. If it hadn't been for Oscar, well, who knows what would have happened?"

"What about Oscar?"

"Evidently he was barking fit to raise the roof."

"No, I mean is he okay?"

"He's alive but in a very poor way. The firemen said they think it started in the kitchen, though they can't be sure until they've investigated further. Oscar couldn't get out — he's shut in there at night — but he was making so much noise that it woke Gloria. She woke her husband and they got out virtually unscathed, but by the time they got him out of the kitchen Oscar was in a state of collapse."

"Where are they all?"

"Gloria and Arnold are in a local hotel. Oscar's in the animal hospital."

"Thank you. Thank you."

Daisy drove straight round to the hotel and found the pair just finishing breakfast.

"Are you all right? I couldn't believe it when I got to the house."

"Thanks to our wonderful boy, yes, we are. I'm sorry, Daisy. I didn't think to call you with so much going on."

Gloria looked awful. She'd obviously managed to get some clothes from somewhere, but her hair was dishevelled and it was obvious she was suffering from shock. Arnold couldn't even bring himself to speak.

"How did it happen? How bad is Oscar?"

Suddenly all three of them were crying.

"They're not sure if he's going to make it, Daisy. I feel like a murderer. If he hadn't been shut in the kitchen, he could have got away without a scratch."

"You weren't to know, Gloria. Nobody expects anything like this to happen. Would it be all right if I went to see him? Is he allowed visitors?"

"We're going there now. You can come with us if you like."

"We'll take my car. Neither of you is in a fit state to drive."

On the way, they filled her in on some more of the details. It had taken two firemen to lift the huge dog and carry him away from further danger. At first they'd thought he was dead, but then he began coughing and wheezing, suffering from severe smoke inhalation.

"With everything else that was going on, one of them still called for an animal ambulance. We saw him yesterday. Oh, Daisy, I'm so frightened we're going to lose him."

Daisy was frightened too, but she had to be strong for the time being. Gloria and Arnold, normally so in control of their lives, were barely holding it together, and it was up to her to take charge. By the time they reached the hospital, she was facing the fact that they all might lose him.

Oscar was on a drip when they arrived. He'd been given oxygen too. There was a gentle wheezing as he breathed.

"There's been no change really, Mrs Clyde. It will take some time before we know if there's been any permanent damage to his lungs but, though we can't make any promises, we're hopeful that he'll pull through. He may not look it at the moment, but Oscar is a fighter."

At the sound of his name, Oscar opened his eyes. They looked a bit glazed, but his tail beat a half-hearted tattoo at the sight of his family. There were more tears, but tinged with a little relief this time. Daisy suddenly remembered she had other commitments.

"Oh my God. The twins and Muffin. I've got to go. Do you want me to take you back?"

"Don't worry," Arnold said, "we'll get a taxi. I think we'd both like to stay with him for a while."

"Can I come back later, after I've walked the others?"

"As long as you're quiet, the presence of any of you will be reassuring for Oscar," the vet said. "His welfare is our main concern now. By all means come back. Is that okay, Mrs Clyde?"

"Of course it is. Daisy is as much Oscar's family as we are."

Daisy kissed Oscar on the top of his head, refrained from telling him he was smelly, and left.

For once in her life, Daisy didn't give her all when walking the dogs. George and Mildred were fine; they had each other to play with, as well as their fan club in the park. Muffin, though, picked up on her mood and the chin to nose lick on Daisy's departure seemed to hold something extra that morning. Driving as quickly as she dared, Daisy found Gloria and Arnold were still at the hospital, waiting for her return. It seemed they didn't want to leave Oscar alone in his pen, and on a busy day there hadn't been someone on the ward every moment during the morning.

"Will you be here for a while, Daisy? We need to get some clothes and a few other essentials. Arnold and I have to talk about what we're going to do next. Obviously we'll stay put in the hotel until Oscar gets better, but he won't be able to come there when he leaves hospital."

"Of course I will, and later I'll go home and get a few things myself. I've got access to the flat for almost three weeks until

Angus's brother arrives. If I stay there, I'll be able to visit Oscar in the mornings when I'd normally be walking with him. That might relieve the pressure on you, if you think it would help. Then I can always come back again in the afternoon to give you a break."

"We're grateful for anything you can do, Daisy. They've been truly amazing here. It's like a normal hospital. Because Oscar's on the critical care ward, we can visit at any time."

Daisy had plenty of time to reflect that afternoon, when she was alone with Oscar. She absentmindedly stroked Oscar's head, as much for her comfort as his, though she wasn't sure he was aware of it until she took her hand away to scratch her nose. He raised his head to look round at her almost reproachfully and settled again when she resumed. The pull on her heart was strong.

She considered phoning Charlie, but thought it would be better to update him face to face. Oscar's condition wasn't something she felt he should hear on the phone, not now that his feelings were as strong as any of theirs.

Daisy phoned before she set out to tell her family what time she'd be home. She was a little disappointed that none of them had questioned her absence. Her mother had been tucked away in her studio, where she inevitably lost track of time, and Mike and Charlie were distracted by the building work.

By the time Daisy reached Home Farm, she was more than grateful that Charlie had prepared supper for them both. Having waited this long, she decided to leave the news until after they'd eaten.

"Good day?" she asked.

"It's been amazing. Non-stop all day. The crew know what they're doing and they didn't seem to mind us hanging around. We missed lunch completely. You know what your mother's like. No sense of time when she's working, and they'd all brought their flasks and sandwiches, so we just did without. How was yours?"

It was time to tell him.

"Not good, Charlie. Awful, in fact."

"Why, what happened?"

She quickly related the events of the day.

"And it didn't occur to you to phone me?" Charlie demanded.

He had spoken very quietly, but he was angrier than she'd ever seen him before, even that morning when he'd found James at her flat.

"Of course it occurred to me. You were busy here, and it took ages anyway before I knew what was going on or even if Oscar was allowed visitors."

"And is he?"

"Yes."

"I'm coming with you tomorrow."

"Actually I'm going back tonight, to the flat. That way, I can get there early in the morning and be around later, after I've walked the twins and Muffin, to give Gloria and Arnold a break. Aren't you needed here?"

"Daisy, if it was the other way round, what would you do?"

"You're right. I'm sorry. I don't suppose there's much you can do at this stage anyway, other than watch, and Dad can do that. Do you want to come with me tonight then?"

"Yes, I do. Can you fill me in on the details while we pack a few things? Just in case we need to stay for a few days."

"I think it's the smoke inhalation that's the biggest threat — that and the shock. If he pulls through, there may be permanent damage to his lungs. He's wheezing a lot. Oh, Charlie, he sounds awful."

"Are they optimistic?"

"Non-committal, but I get the impression they think he'll pull through. They just don't know if there'll be any lasting effects."

"He's a fighter, though, I'm sure."

"Yes, they said as much."

"I couldn't bear it if we lost him."

"No."

"What's the matter with me? I haven't even asked about Gloria and Arnold. What kind of a person am I?"

"One who's received a big shock. They're okay. Very shaken but basically intact. They're staying at the hotel in the village for the time being, but they'll have to decide what to do soon. When Oscar's well enough to leave hospital, he won't be allowed to stay there. They're not thinking straight yet. They could rent somewhere, I suppose, until they buy a new place."

Charlie was very quiet for a few moments.

"He'll be all right, Charlie. You wait until tomorrow, then you'll see. Are you ready to go?"

"Yes, we'll just stop at the house to tell your parents and then we can be off. We'll stay as long as we're needed. Mike can supervise things while we're away."

CHAPTER TWENTY-ONE

First thing next morning, Daisy and Charlie were in the waiting room at the animal hospital.

"Oscar's had a comfortable night, but he'll be with us for a few days for sure," said the vet. "Would you like to see him now?"

They followed the nurse into the room where Daisy had seen Oscar the day before. He appeared to be sleeping, but when they approached and quietly called his name, he began thumping with his tail. Charlie opened the catch on the pen and stroked his head as Daisy had the day before.

"Hello, old boy. Got yourself into the wars, have you? Don't worry. It'll be okay."

He and Daisy continued speaking softly to him until Gloria and Arnold arrived, and they sat together until the vet had finished with her current patient.

"He's a very lucky boy. If he'd been smaller, he might not have made it. I'm pretty sure he'll be home with you in a few days, but now he's out of danger, it might be an idea not to visit quite so much. Once a day will be fine. Give him a chance to get as much rest as he can. That's what he needs now."

Daisy and Charlie got up to leave, and Gloria asked if they could meet them for lunch at the hotel after walking the other dogs.

"There's something we'd like to talk to you about," she said.

"Of course. We'll see you later then," Daisy said, waving goodbye.

A short while later, Daisy and Charlie were sitting on a bench in the park while George and Mildred played chase.

"They must want to talk about their move," said Daisy. "You don't think they'll leave Blackheath, do you?" There was a hint of alarm in her voice.

"Why would they?"

"No reason I can think of. Anyway, there's no point in trying to guess. We'll soon find out. Yes, George, I can see you've had enough. Time to take you home."

Once home, the dogs flung themselves into their basket, ready for a well-deserved sleep. Daisy, unable to resist, took a photo and they left to collect Muffin. She seemed to be moving every single muscle in excitement as they opened the door. Luckily, Daisy had quick reactions, catching the little dog as she leapt into her arms.

"Did you think we weren't coming? We're only a few minutes late."

Daisy continued to make soothing noises, carrying Muffin to collect her lead, an action which only caused her to wriggle even more. There was quite a breeze blowing by the time they got to the park again, so Charlie and Daisy walked quite briskly and in relative silence. In spite of it being a dry day, Muffin managed to find a dirty puddle to play in. They were convinced it was because she wanted the pleasure of a bath, something she'd always loved. Back at her house, after lots of blowing and chasing of bubbles they rubbed her down and left her to settle. It was time for lunch.

"We've been talking a lot over the last couple of days," said Gloria when they were all seated in the hotel restaurant. "Not much else to do when you have no home to go to, and they won't let us back to work yet. They told us both to take the week off. We're grateful, of course, but actually it would be easier if we had something to do now they don't want us to sit with Oscar all day."

"I know what you mean. Nice as it is, it must be very difficult here," Daisy replied.

"It's not just Oscar and the fire. There's something else we've been trying to reach a decision on for several weeks now."

Daisy and Charlie both looked at her expectantly. Arnold was sitting very quietly.

"Six weeks ago, Arnold was offered a huge promotion. We didn't know whether to take it because it means relocating to New York."

Daisy's heart sank. "What!"

"There were only a few days left for us to decide when the fire happened. We'd more or less made up our minds to stay put." The pain was clear to see on Gloria's face. "We weren't able to have children. Oscar has been our child for over six years now, and the thought of leaving him behind wasn't even to be considered. We'd have an apartment in New York, not the place to keep a dog like that, even if they'd let us. Not only that, he's no youngster any more, not for a dog his size. I suppose you can see where I'm going with this."

"Not exactly, Gloria, no."

"Daisy, you've known Oscar for almost as long as we have. Our minds seem to have been made up for us, with this fire. It would take months to find and move into somewhere new. We'd have to rent for a while and then, well…"

Arnold picked up as Gloria's words were left hanging in the air. "What she's trying to say is, this job offer is an opportunity we'd be crazy to turn down. We would have, though, if it hadn't been for what's happened. As it is, it would seem the choice has been made for us. We just don't feel we can do it to Oscar, change his home, his country, and make a long plane journey. Not after what he's been through. He needs to feel settled."

Daisy couldn't believe they would let Oscar go, though she could see he was their first consideration. She wondered what was coming next. She looked from Arnold to Gloria.

"We'd like you to take him. It was out of the question while you were still in your flat. Naturally you were our first and obvious choice, but your circumstances were wrong. Now that you're living in the country, well, it would help ease the blow to know Oscar was with you and could live the life he deserves."

Charlie and Daisy both sat in stunned silence. Of all the scenarios either might have imagined, this was not one of them.

Finally, Daisy responded. "I can't begin to imagine how hard this must be for you both. We'd love to have him. You know that. I promise we will do everything we can to give him the best time."

It went very quiet for a few moments. Nobody knew what to say. Then Arnold lifted his glass.

"A toast. To Oscar."

"To Oscar."

After visiting Oscar briefly later that afternoon, Daisy and Charlie returned to Kent. They would pop in to see him for a short while each day when they walked the others, but there was no longer any need to stay in London. Apart from anything else, both thought it best to give Gloria and Arnold as much time with him as they could.

Mike was outside when they pulled into the drive. "How's Oscar?" he asked.

"He's out of the woods, they think, but it'll be a while before he's well enough to leave hospital. Is Mum painting? I know it's a bit of a cheek, but as it's Tuesday and we missed lunch we were wondering if we might come for supper."

"Yes, she is, and of course come for supper. I'm sure I'll be able to rustle up something."

"How's it gone today, Mike?" Charlie asked, nodding his head at the building site.

"A lot of comings and goings. I think the utilities people want to get their pipes and cables laid before the weather changes. Once they've run those, I believe they seal them off until the structural work is done and connect it all much further down the line. I've not been involved with anything like this before. A bit of painting and wallpapering is all I've ever done. I'm sure the project manager knows what he's doing."

"Yes, I agree. The reason I want to be here is in case something comes up that would cause a hold-up if they needed to ask us about it," said Charlie.

Daisy gave him a look that told him she knew there was more to it than that.

"Okay, you're right," he conceded. "I'm excited. I want to see it and feel it."

"There's an old building set in the loft, if you want to play," Daisy teased. "Do you remember, Dad, when you used to drag it out because you were sure I'd enjoy it? Talk about using me as an excuse!"

"I'd forgotten all about that. What do you think, Charlie? Shall I see if I can find it?"

"I was joking, Dad."

"No, it's a great idea. Would you like me to climb up there and have a look?"

Daisy looked from one to the other in disbelief, cast her gaze heavenwards and went to find her mother.

In spite of Mike insisting he'd only gathered leftovers together, they sat down in the kitchen faced with a huge spread. Sorry as she felt for Gloria and Arnold, Daisy couldn't help but be excited when she told her parents the news about Oscar.

"Do you think it's time for you to reconsider, kitten?" asked Mike.

"Daddy, how can you say that? You know how much he means to me."

"Not Oscar, the others. If you think of the time involved when you could be working here, it's hardly viable to be driving backwards and forwards, particularly now that Oscar will be an expense rather than a source of income."

Daisy felt deflated. It was something she'd thought of, of course, but she didn't want to face the idea of parting from Muffin and the twins.

"You'll have plenty of time to make up your mind. It will be weeks before you can do anything here other than follow up with your old customers and maybe deliver some flyers. Meirah, do you think you could design a suitable one? Put the word out that we'll be ready for business, with a bit of luck, by Christmas. Maybe it would be better to cut the cord with the others, Daisy. Hopefully they will be able to spend their holidays here when their owners go away, but meanwhile, shouldn't you give them a chance to find someone else?"

Unable to answer, Daisy's chest filled with sadness, because she knew what her dad said made sense.

Daisy received a phone call a few days later.

"Daisy, it's Gloria. They've told us we can collect Oscar on Monday. I can't believe he's been there for a week! Anyway, we're going to say our goodbyes tomorrow, as we can't bring him back here."

Gloria and Arnold were still at the hotel, and they'd been spending the time there making arrangements to move to the States.

"You'll appreciate we don't have much to take with us. Everything we owned went up with the house, so Arnold's company is expediting the move and dealing with visas, that sort of thing. We're off ourselves on Tuesday. To be quite honest, I'll be glad of something to do, you know, to take my mind off our boy."

"We'll do the very best we can for him, Gloria. You know that."

"I do. It's the only way I've been able to reconcile myself to the situation. Will it be all right for you to collect him on Monday? I'll leave his papers there, and I've given them your address so they can change the microchip."

"Of course. We'll get him after we've walked the others. I think the trip back here will be enough exercise for one day, and there's plenty of room for him to move around if he wants to."

"You'll keep in touch, won't you? Let us know how he is?"

"I was just going to ask you to send contact details. I can't thank you enough, Gloria, but I can promise you he'll be well looked after."

During the previous week, Daisy had arranged for the contractors on site to fence in an area around the bungalow. With so much going on and otherwise unrestricted access to the lane, Oscar would at least have an area to play in. She didn't trust him, once he was better, not to go bounding off somewhere and get himself hurt. She'd mentioned it to Gloria as well, hoping it would be another little reassurance for her.

Daisy had done a lot of soul-searching since Mike's suggestion the previous Tuesday. Charlie, sensibly, had kept well out of it. He had bonded with Oscar most strongly, and it wasn't for him to interfere between Daisy and the others. In the end she'd come to the conclusion that she had little choice. The new business would need her complete attention if they were to make a success of it. Even then, they expected to be very quiet for the first few months, until they managed to build up a good reputation. Her father had invested his land, Charlie his money. It was only fair that she gave every moment she could — that was her part of the bargain.

George and Mildred's owners were sad but understanding when Daisy said she would have to give up walking the dogs at Christmas time. Muffin's owner Eunice was distraught. Daisy had looked after Muffin since she was a puppy. Fortunately, Daisy had friends in the dog-walking world and was able to recommend a replacement. She was careful to promote someone the dogs already knew from their daily trips to the park so it wouldn't be entirely strange to them.

"I know I'm doing the right thing, so why don't I feel better?" she asked Charlie on the way to collect Oscar.

"Because you've just been out with them. Because everything seemed normal. Because you can't imagine not seeing them every day. I wouldn't like you very much if you did feel better. You need time to adjust, just as they will."

By this time they'd reached the veterinary hospital, and all Daisy's thoughts turned to Oscar. He was looking much better than when they'd last seen him on Friday, and as they produced his lead he started to bounce and turn in circles, not an easy feat in the restricted space available. They were handed his papers, along with other important documents.

Oscar sat on the back seat of the car, his nose raised to the two-inch crack they'd left in the window for his benefit, looking for all the world as if he was off on an adventure.

CHAPTER TWENTY-TWO

When they arrived home, Daisy let Oscar off his lead in the new enclosure and he tore around for several minutes, sniffing here and digging there until he flopped to the ground with his tongue hanging out. After he'd had a few minutes to recover, they took him into the bungalow to introduce him to his new bed and a couple of toys. He very quickly curled up on his new bed and went to sleep.

"It's not like him at all. He loves to play. Do you think he's okay?" asked Charlie.

"Charlie, he's been confined for over a week," Daisy replied. "It'll take quite a while before he's fully recovered. Look how long it took me, and I wasn't nearly as ill as he's been. He'll be okay. Just give him a bit of time."

The next day Gillian, who had been invited to Tuesday lunch, renewed her acquaintance with Oscar. She was pleased to see him, but it seemed to everyone that she had something on her mind. They were sitting at the table drinking coffee when Gillian put down her cup and looked directly at Meirah.

"Is there something you haven't told me?" Gillian's words sounded like a challenge. The others were baffled, but it appeared Meirah knew immediately what Gillian was referring to.

"It never seemed like the right time to tell you. How did you find out?"

"I phoned James. I'd decided I wanted to make the break formal, so I told him I was going to contact my solicitor to initiate divorce proceedings. I thought he'd be over the moon. Legally he would probably be entitled to a lot more than the allowance I was giving him, so I couldn't understand his reaction at all, not at first. It was only when I thought about it for a while that a possible explanation presented itself."

"It must have come as a shock after all this time."

"It doesn't really matter to me anymore. My only concern is the impact it might have on the children."

The two younger members of the family were looking curious now.

"Would you like to tell them, or shall I?" said Gillian.

Meirah took a deep breath. "Well, Mike already knows, obviously. There wasn't very much I could do. I didn't know where James had gone. Australia's a big place. I needed to think about me and Daisy. It didn't really make any difference then, one way or the other. Then I met Mike. It wasn't important to either of us. We just wanted to be together."

Charlie looked from one woman to the other. The penny was beginning to drop.

"You were never divorced," he said slowly. "And James married Mum. On top of everything else, he's a bigamist as well."

"I'm so sorry, Charlie!"

"Seems fairly typical to me. He'd do almost anything to get what he wants. I don't suppose Kirsty will be bothered. We've all pretty much given up on him." Charlie began to laugh.

"What's so funny?" Daisy asked him.

"I love the poetic justice of it. He can't go ahead with divorce proceedings because if he does, he'll go to prison. No wonder he's tried so hard to get a decent allowance from you.

It's priceless. At least the bastard can't take you for half of what you own. Well done, Mum."

Sam came to visit Daisy later that week. Since Niall was away in Birmingham for work, she was staying with Meirah and Mike in the main house for a couple of days.

"My God, you're huge!" Daisy exclaimed when she saw her friend. "You look like you've got a football team in there."

"Only the two, Daisy. You know, I'd forgotten how beautiful it is out here, even with all that noise and mess going on," Sam said, looking away from the work and out onto the countryside. The horses had been moved to another paddock at a distance from the centre of activity and could be seen grazing contentedly.

It was early October, and Sam had only five weeks to go before the babies arrived. She'd begun maternity leave a week earlier with the intention of going back to work if she had to, but she'd confided in Daisy that she'd sooner spend the first three or so years at home with the twins if she could.

"Can we go for a walk around the farm, do you think? It seems a shame to miss this lovely sunshine, even if it's cold," said Sam.

At the sound of the word 'walk', Oscar raised his chin from where it was resting on his front paws.

"The ground's a bit uneven in places, Sam. Would you like to walk in the lane instead?" Daisy asked.

"No, but I can see your logic," Sam replied with a sigh. "What do you think, Oscar? Shall I get your lead?"

Oscar liked people who understood his language. He put a huge paw on Sam's knee and looked at her approvingly.

Once they were ready, they turned into the lane towards open countryside, where the stream that ran at the back of Home Farm meandered round and under a small footbridge. They crossed over and onto the path that followed the water's edge. Daisy knew it to be well-trodden and flat. Releasing Oscar from his lead, they walked for a while until Daisy gestured to a fallen tree trunk. "Would you like a rest, Sam?" she asked.

"Yes, I'm ready to sit down. I keep forgetting I'm carrying three of us instead of one. Look at Oscar. Doesn't he just love it here?"

Daisy and Charlie had walked this way many times with him and he knew it well, but there were still hundreds of things he needed to investigate. He never went far, bounding back every few minutes to make sure they were okay before setting off again. With no lasting damage to his lungs, he'd embraced his new life with all the exuberance of a puppy.

As they rose to continue their walk, Sam clutched at her stomach.

"Oh no! It can't be," she gasped.

But of course it could. It wasn't unusual for twins to arrive early. Unfortunately, Daisy didn't have any signal on her phone. She called Oscar, clipped on his lead and tied him to a branch. He sat at Sam's feet, resting his head against her while Daisy rushed off to find somewhere she could use her phone or, worst scenario, run back home, call for help and get the car.

"I won't be long, Sam. It's fifteen minutes max back to the farm. Nothing's going to happen in that time. Oscar will look after you."

Sam wasn't sure what Oscar was expected to do, but his presence calmed her. Daisy was as good as her promise, bringing Charlie with her. He lifted Sam effortlessly and carried her along the footpath to the road, where they'd left the car.

"I'm impressed. In future, I shall refer to you as Superman," Sam managed to joke.

"Any more contractions?" he asked.

"Only one."

"I think we'd better take you straight to hospital, just to be on the safe side. Daisy, tell me which way to go."

Fortunately, the twins weren't in quite as much of a hurry as they'd thought. Nevertheless, all Sam's carefully laid plans for their birth were scrapped when she was laid up in a country hospital instead of the one she'd been attending throughout her pregnancy. Daisy phoned Niall as soon as they got to the hospital. He jumped straight in the car, having for once driven to Birmingham, and after an amazingly uneventful journey he arrived within twenty minutes of the birth of his son, followed five minutes later by a daughter.

"Did you have to be in such a hurry, Sam?" he teased. "We haven't even decided on their names yet."

"No, you're wrong there, Niall. The decision's been made for us. If it's okay with you, they have to be Charlie and Daisy."

Two days later, Sam and Niall's parents all arrived, anxious to see their first grandchildren. None had intended to stay over, but Daisy's parents were adamant they stay at the house.

When Daisy went to visit Sam, she found her friend looking tired but radiant.

"Look at you! You're amazing."

"Would you like to hold the babies?" asked Sam.

"Can I? Are you sure?"

"Yes. They're doing well. Charlie's a little bit behind, but both were a decent birth weight."

As Daisy cradled each baby in turn, she said, "It's not surprising I thought you had a football team in there. They look tiny now, but I still don't know how you managed to fit them both in there. They're beautiful, Sam. We're thrilled you named them after us, and Charlie was bursting with pride when you said you wanted him to be their godfather."

"Some things just seem right, don't they?"

When the babies were back in their cots, they chatted for a few minutes but Sam's eyes were drooping, so Daisy left, promising to come again the next day.

The following morning, after walking Muffin, Mildred and George, Daisy stopped at the giant shopping mall on the west Kent border to look for something for her godchildren. As she picked her way through tiny clothes, she found something stirring inside her that she'd never suspected was there.

This could have been me, buying things for my own baby, she thought. *I'm nearly thirty. It isn't going to happen, is it? No-one's going to make me feel about them the way I do about Charlie.*

Daisy had been struggling for weeks with her emotions. She'd been able to convince herself she could spend her life working side by side with the man she loved. There was a naturalness that made it possible on one level to be completely at ease but, on another, every nerve ending was screaming how she felt about him.

When she got home and showed Charlie what she'd bought, he was absolutely delighted and had her in a fit of giggles, putting one of the tiny mittens on the little fingers of his enormous hands. Those hands were particularly dextrous, she found, when they wrapped the presents.

"It's not fair. You can even do those tiny little satin bows."

"I learnt how when Kirsty was little. Mum can't do them either, and James certainly wasn't interested. It was up to me, Christmas and birthdays, to wrap everything for Kirsty."

They went to the hospital together later that day and presented Sam with their gifts. Her fingers hovered over the packages.

"You want to wait for Niall, don't you?" said Daisy.

"Is it that obvious? Do you mind?"

"Of course not. I'd be the same."

CHAPTER TWENTY-THREE

A week later, Sam and her family went back to London and things at Home Farm reverted to what passed for normal at the present time. Then, early in November, unprecedentedly bad weather struck the southeast corner of the country and everything ground to a halt. Daisy could find no way of getting to Blackheath and had to phone to give her apologies. Glad she could call upon her successor, who lived locally to her charges, she realised how impractical it was to continue in the way she had been and made a difficult decision. A few days later, she phoned Muffin's owner, Eunice.

"Eunice, I don't know what you think and I'm quite happy to come back just for a little while, but it seems to make more sense for Katherine to carry on, now that Muffin's got used to her. We could easily have another bout of bad weather between now and Christmas, and then she'd have to adjust all over again."

"I can't believe it's coming to an end," said Eunice sadly. "You're right, of course, but I can't believe we won't see you again. It doesn't seem possible."

"I have no intention of not seeing Muffin again, or you for that matter. Whenever you go away, Muffin will have a holiday home here with us, free of charge. We'll throw in a cup of tea for you as well."

Daisy then had a similar conversation with George and Mildred's owners and swallowed hard as she finished the call. It was the end of an era.

"Everyone seems to be busy at the moment. Do you fancy a walk?" Mike asked Daisy. She knew her father realised how hard it had been for her, severing those last ties with Blackheath.

"That would be lovely, Daddy. Shall we take Oscar?"

"Hasn't he already been out today?"

"Yes, but he's always ready for another walk."

"Not this time, Daisy. There's something I want to talk to you about."

There was a crease between his eyes that told her he was troubled.

"Okay, I'll just get my coat."

In the end they just walked down to the stream, taking a couple of folding chairs from Meirah's outbuilding.

"What is it, Daddy? You're not ill, are you? Or Mum?"

"No, nothing like that, kitten. This is more about you."

Daisy waited. The silence was loud in her ears until Mike began.

"How long have you felt the way you do about Charlie?"

As far as bombshells went, it was a cracker.

"I don't know what you mean."

"I've known you since you were a baby. I've seen you happy. I've seen you sad. I've never seen you in love before."

It seemed the pretence was over, as far as her father was concerned. "Oh, Daddy, what am I going to do? It was almost from the beginning. Like someone had waved a magic wand and there was my Prince Charming, only it was the Wicked Fairy and she said I couldn't have him. Does Mummy know?"

"She hasn't said anything, and naturally I haven't mentioned it to her. Whatever possessed you to go into business with him?"

"He asked me."

"You can do better than that."

"There isn't ever going to be anyone else for me. After Jonathan I realised that. I don't want second best. So on the one hand Charlie presented me with my life's dream, and on the other he took away any chance I ever had of finding happiness with another man."

"And do you think you made the right decision?"

"There was only ever the one. How long have you known?"

"Only since Sam had the babies. I wasn't sure at first. It's in the occasional glance, like you can't help yourself. If you were still living in Blackheath I might have thought I was imagining it, but seeing you every day confirmed it. There was no mistake."

"Would anyone else be able to tell?" Daisy asked him, horrified at the thought that Charlie might have noticed.

"I don't think so. Only your mother, maybe."

They sat in silence for a few minutes, just watching little silver fish racing along in the stream at their feet.

"It's not too late, you know. You can back out if you want to. Say you're not ready and run off to see Kirsty or something like that."

"And leave you here with this mess?"

"It isn't a mess, Daisy. Don't ever think that. You're not the only one who likes Charlie. I'm more than happy for the business to be here, and we could employ someone to do your job."

"I don't know, Daddy. At least if I stay I have part of the dream."

"I just don't want to see you in pain, kitten. If I'm honest, I don't want you to go. Life has suddenly taken a wonderful turn for me, something I never expected at my age, but this isn't about me. This isn't a six-month project. This is a life-commitment. Are you really equipped to deal with it, given the circumstances? I'll stand by you, whatever you decide."

"I know you will, Daddy. I'll think about it."

In some ways, it was a relief that her father knew. It didn't really alter anything. Daisy meant it when she said she'd think about it, but it was a no-brainer. Part of the dream was better than none. Things were moving quickly now. She and Charlie had talked about what to call the kennels many times, but it always came back to Shepherds in the plural because they had a common surname. Mike had long since declared he didn't want that kind of recognition.

"In any case, Shepherds and Foster will just make everyone think they're coming to a brewery."

Plans for the logo and fascia had originally been dotted with a number of breed sketches, but they'd abandoned that idea.

"There are far too many to include them all. It just looks a mess," Meirah said, looking at the mock-up. "And I don't think adding paws as a signature will add anything. 'Boarding Kennels and Grooming Parlour' will tell anyone passing what they need to know. For the rest, if you do your marketing properly, you won't need pretty pictures."

"I had no idea you possessed such business acumen, Meirah. Is there anything else you'd like to tell us?" Charlie teased.

"No, you're doing fine at the moment, Charlie, and you've been in business for long enough not to need my advice." She laughed. "But if there is anything, I'll be sure to let you know."

November was drawing to a close, and against all the odds it looked like they'd be ready by Christmas. Empty, but ready.

In early December, Daisy received a call from one of her old clients.

"Is that Daisy? It's Stephanie Webb — do you remember me? You used to walk my Billy."

"Of course I remember you. How are you?"

"My second child is about to start nursery part-time in January, and I'll be going back to work three mornings a week. We've all heard about the new place, but I was just wondering if you'd have time to do walking as well. I know it isn't what you've advertised."

"I hadn't thought…"

"I pass Home Farm on the way to school. I could just drop Billy in and you could keep him until it's time to collect Charlotte. He's getting on a bit, so he wouldn't be much trouble. Only, by the time I get home from work, I'll want to spend time with Charlotte. I can't believe she's old enough to go to school already."

"I suppose I could exercise him here on the farm. There's plenty of room, and it'll be lovely to have him again. Yes, of course. January, you said?"

"Yes, and we'd like to go and visit my parents over Christmas as well, only Billy doesn't get on with their cat. Will you be open by then? Can I book Billy in for a week?"

"Of course you can. Do you want to drop him in for a couple of hours one day, so it's not completely strange when the time comes to leave him?"

"That would be fantastic. Thank you, Daisy. Lovely to have you back."

Daisy put down the phone and went looking for Charlie. "Charlie! *Charlie*! We've got our first customer."

Stephanie Webb spread the word. Two more bookings came in for the Christmas period, together with a desperate plea from a local couple who worked full-time.

"She's only a puppy. We thought if we walked her every morning and evening, she'd be okay. We didn't want to leave her shut in the kitchen, but she's so bored she's resorted to eating the furniture."

Daisy knew it was quite a common problem. Many well-meaning people believed that exercising their dog meant it would sleep all day.

"Do you do daycare as well as boarding? So she's got some company. You wouldn't have to walk her or anything like that. We enjoy taking her out."

"Yes, of course. We'd be happy to. We've got a dedicated paddock where our daycare dogs can play, and there are kennels to put them if needs be," Daisy said, thinking on her feet and looking across the table at Mike. The paddock where the horses had been moved from was adjacent to the kennel block. She was pretty sure Mike wouldn't mind.

"You want to start straight away?"

"If possible. Because of the furniture chewing we've had to shut her in the kitchen, and that's just not fair to her."

"That shouldn't be a problem. There's still some internal work going on, but that won't interfere with us having … what's her name, your puppy?"

"Buttons. She's a tan-coloured terrier, but she's got three black spots in a line on her chest that make her look as if she's wearing a waistcoat."

"How lovely. What time will you be dropping her off?"

"Is seven-thirty in the morning too early? We have to get to work, you see."

"No, it's fine. We're always up at the crack of dawn here. See you tomorrow then."

Daisy filled everyone in on what she had arranged.

"I didn't think you'd mind, Dad, as the paddock is just sitting there doing nothing at the moment."

"Quite the opposite. I'm full of admiration for your ingenuity, and it's a great idea. Where one goes others may follow."

"I've been thinking as well," said Meirah, "that if we've got the room we might as well maximise its use. There's an area at one end of the building you haven't allocated anything to yet. Why not convert it into a veterinary clinic?"

"That's a fantastic idea!" Mike looked at Charlie. "What do you think? It shouldn't be too difficult to knock out that window and make it into a door. That way, there'd be a dedicated entrance. It could be an attached but completely separate entity."

"Definitely possible. Aren't there already enough vets around here, though?"

"There isn't a small animal clinic in the immediate area. We could rent it fully-equipped or hire a locum. I'm for it."

Daisy looked round at them all. Her eyes were sparkling. They'd never expected to get any bookings any time soon, possibly not for several weeks, and here they were with three already and their first daycare dog coming in the very next day. It was going to be a Christmas to remember.

CHAPTER TWENTY-FOUR

Later that day, Charlie was relaxing in Meirah and Mike's kitchen when the phone rang. As he reached for it, he said, "Let's hope this is another booking."

He frowned when he answered and heard his mother's panicked voice.

"I can't hear you, Mum. Slow down."

"It's Kirsty. There's been an accident. She's in hospital. Charlie, she's on life support. They don't know if she's going to make it!"

The others watched as the blood drained from Charlie's face.

"Have you arranged your flight yet? No? Good. Don't worry, I'll do it from here. I'm coming with you."

"What about your business?"

"They'll just have to manage without me. Daisy knows what she's doing. There's no way I'm staying here. Now, let me get off the phone and I'll call you back as soon as I've made a booking."

Charlie looked at their expectant faces and filled them in immediately.

"Kirsty and Cam went to Cairns for a long weekend. She's been stung by a jellyfish. She's in hospital on a life support system."

"I'm coming with you," said Daisy immediately.

"No, Daisy, you can't. You heard what I said to Mum. You're needed here."

"But she's my sister too."

"I know, but I really don't think we have a choice. I've got to make that booking now. We'll talk about it later."

It didn't take long. Before they knew it, he was phoning Gillian back.

"Can you leave within the hour?" he asked.

"Of course I can."

"Okay, I'll meet you there. Terminal five." He gave her the details and went to the bungalow to throw a few things into a bag. Daisy went with him.

"At least let me drive you to the airport," she begged.

He looked up from his packing, his face filled with pain at the thought of leaving her, pain at the anticipation of what he might find on the other side of the world. He hugged her. "Thank you, Daisy. I don't think I'm in a fit state to drive, and I couldn't bear to sit in the back of a taxi, alone with my thoughts."

In the car they talked about Kirsty for a few minutes, but as there was nothing they could do and the conversation filled them both with grief, they discussed work instead, grateful to have something to distract them. The journey was uneventful, and soon Daisy was dropping Charlie at the terminal building. She parked the car and hurried back to wait with him and Gillian for as long as she could before they went into the departure lounge. They were standing in the queue, checking in the luggage when she got back.

"I wish I was coming with you," she said to Gillian.

"I know. I wish you were too. It's funny, isn't it? When you're in business, no matter what problems arise, you have some sort of control. This is completely out of my hands and I don't know how to deal with it."

"Which is why it's a good thing Charlie's going with you. Give Kirsty my love, will you, and tell her I said she has to get better quickly. She's getting married in a few months, and she promised I could come to her wedding."

CHAPTER TWENTY-FIVE

It was shortly after take-off that Gillian grabbed Charlie's arm.

"What's the matter, Mum? You've never been bothered about flying before."

"It's not that. I've just realised I didn't call James. He has absolutely no idea what's going on."

For all Charlie cared it could stay that way. James had never shown much affection for his daughter, so why should it be any different now? On the other hand, it was an added concern for Gillian, and that he did care about.

"We can call from Singapore when we refuel. Don't worry, he can catch another plane. He won't be that far behind us."

"It might be…"

Gillian left the sentence incomplete, but Charlie finished it in his mind. *Too late by then.*

"She's going to pull through this, Mum. She's going to be okay."

He wished he felt as confident as he sounded, but Gillian looked at least a tiny bit reassured.

In the airport terminal in Singapore, Gillian was pacing up and down so quickly that Charlie, whose legs were considerably longer than hers, was having difficulty keeping up with her. She had just got off the phone with James.

"How could he? The man is unbelievable!" she spat.

"What did he say, Mum?"

"He said, and I quote, 'I'm sure she'll be okay. Give her my love and tell her to get well soon.' Can you believe it?"

He could, but thought it politic not to say so. He managed to persuade her to have coffee and a sandwich while they waited and even had one himself.

"I'm not hungry."

"Neither am I, but we won't do Kirsty any good if we arrive in a state of collapse."

Charlie called Daisy to keep her updated, then before they knew it he and Gillian were on their way again. It seemed an interminable journey. When they arrived at Sydney, they had to catch an internal flight to Cairns. In spite of themselves they'd both drifted into a fitful sleep on the Singapore to Australia leg, but neither woke refreshed. They felt desperately tired as they boarded the final plane. Then they took a taxi straight from the airport to the hospital.

"How is she, Cam? Can we see her?" Gillian asked as soon as they'd been shown to the right ward.

"Yes, but be prepared. She hasn't woken up since it happened. They said that's not a bad thing, that her body has internalised to fight the infection, but I can see they're worried."

Gillian went into Kirsty's room and held her hand for a few moments before rushing out. Charlie went after her. She was standing outside, with tears racing down her cheeks.

"I can't bear it. What if she doesn't pull through? What if she dies, Charlie?"

Charlie, who was fighting to control his own fears, said, "You need to be brave, Mum. Hold her hand and tell her she's going to get better. If you believe it, then she will too."

"I don't know how Cam's managed. It must have been almost two days now."

"He's a great guy."

"Can we go back in now?"

"Can you hold it together?"

"For Kirsty's sake, I must." She frowned. "I can't believe James, I really can't."

"I can. You go in. I'll follow in a minute. I promised I'd phone Daisy as soon as we got here. They must be on tenterhooks at Home Farm."

Daisy picked up the phone straight away. "Charlie, thank goodness. How is she? Is she going to be okay?"

"We've not been here long. I've been in to see her and she seems to be in a coma. Cam said something about her body internalising, but I don't know if there's any truth in that. Daisy, I can't tell Mum, but I'm terrified. She looks so tiny and pale."

"I wish I could be there. I don't want to put any added pressure on you, but please call as often as possible. It's the silence that's so hard to deal with, the not knowing."

"You'll be sick of the sound of my voice soon. It's only being able to talk to you that stops me from breaking down in front of Mum. Even that quick call from Singapore was a help."

"Well, it helped me too. I'll tell Mum and Dad. In the meantime, they send their love. Love you."

"Love you too."

Neither even stopped to consider what they might mean by that.

Gillian and Charlie maintained their vigil at Kirsty's bedside. There was no way Cam could be persuaded to take a break, so Charlie went out and bought him some shaving gear and packed him off to the toilets to freshen up.

"If you really want to marry my sister, you'll do it. Have you looked at yourself? If she wakes up sees you like that, the whole thing will be off, and that's aside from giving her a relapse." Trying to joke maybe wasn't appropriate, but for Charlie it was his default coping mechanism. When Cam returned, he said, "A vast improvement. I can almost appreciate what she sees in you."

Cam groaned loudly and Charlie pulled him close, both men breaking down in tears.

"She's going to be all right, Cam," Charlie murmured. "If the worst was going to happen, it would have done so already. I know it's hard to believe, looking at her now, but I'm sure she's gathering her resources in the fight to beat this thing."

"The doctors and nurses did actually say that," said Cam. "I'm going to believe them. I *have* to believe them. The alternative is unimaginable."

"Go on, then. Now you're looking a bit more respectable, go and sit with Kirsty. I'm going out to get us all some sandwiches, which you will eat," he added as he saw Cam was about to protest. "Any preferences?"

"No, whatever you're having will be fine."

Daisy had been delighted with little Buttons when she'd arrived the morning after Charlie had left. She reminded her of George and Mildred. The little dog took to Daisy immediately, and stuck to her heel for most of the day. Oscar, who obviously felt that exercise was something to be taken in moderation, raised his head occasionally to look at this new distraction before sliding back into a dream that had his nose and closed eyes twitching. Daisy hoped it was a good dream. She felt she was living in a waking nightmare, and being busy was her way of coping.

185

She picked up Oscar's lead to take him and Buttons across to the now beautifully finished grooming parlour. Grooming an animal of Oscar's size was no easy task, and was not helped by the fact that he thought it was a game. She put a halter round his neck to keep him steady, knowing full well he would otherwise be on the ground with his legs in the air, waiting for his tummy to be rubbed. Buttons watched with interest for a while and then went for a wander around the room until Mike came looking for Daisy and opened the door. Buttons made a quick exit between his legs and they spent the next ten minutes catching her.

Once both dogs were back in hand, Daisy and Mike made their way to the other end of the building, to where Meirah had suggested they house the proposed veterinary surgery.

"There's plenty of room, that's for sure," said Mike.

"And you wouldn't mind, Dad, another business on site?"

"To tell you the truth, Daisy, I'm really excited about the whole project. I think I'd become a little complacent, too ready to slip into semi-retirement."

"You're definitely not ready for that, and Mum certainly won't ever give up painting. I'd rather imagined you opening your own restaurant."

"Too much like hard work. No, this way I can be around, help when I'm needed and enjoy watching the whole thing evolve. And have my lovely daughter around all the time."

"Speaking of daughters, did I tell you what Charlie said when he phoned from Singapore? James isn't even going to see Kirsty. He sent his love and said get well soon."

"It seems he's not too interested in either of his daughters."

"I'm glad he left, Daddy. Otherwise, I wouldn't have had you, and I know which I'd prefer."

"Well, it's nice to be appreciated," Mike said, more than a little touched.

"Oh, it's not you, it's your cooking," Daisy teased, trying to lighten the mood. "So, what do we think? Is the veterinary surgery a good idea?"

"I think it's a great idea. Your mother's head isn't always in the clouds. Let's do it."

With Christmas fast approaching they managed to get a quote, but work wouldn't begin until they were into the New Year. Mike advertised for a vet and they were inundated with applications. He and Daisy decided to start interviewing immediately. The conversion wouldn't take long once it began, and anyone leasing the premises would presumably have to give notice. In Charlie's absence, Daisy and Mike decided to rent out the surgery, and the sooner it was up and running, the better.

"If we offer a six-month lease, we'll know by then if we want to employ someone and run it ourselves or just take the income from the rent. As long as we have some input as to how it functions, it's probably better to leave it as an independent business. The biggest asset will be having it on site," said Daisy.

Mike agreed. "The equipment will be a large investment, and we'd have to wait a long time for a decent return, but we need to look at the bigger picture. A surgery on the premises will bring in ancillary business, so with that and the rent we'd be recouping our expenditure that way."

"I think we'll find it's the best way to go. We'll have enough on our plate running the kennels and the grooming parlour. But I'd be very disappointed if the knock-on effect of having a veterinary clinic on the premises wasn't substantial."

Daisy sat at the table in her parents' kitchen one morning, nursing a cup of coffee. They were discussing arrangements for Christmas.

"I can't say I feel much like celebrating, Mummy. I thought we'd at least have Gillian and Charlie here this year. Looks like it's just the three of us."

"Don't you talk like that, my girl!" Meirah protested. "We've had plenty of Christmases when it's just been us, and it's always been wonderful, except maybe the year your dad tripped over the coffee table and blew his cover as Santa Claus."

"I was devastated. I'd truly believed in the whole thing until then."

"I've never seen you cry such big tears!" Mike groaned.

"Yes, but you comforted me, Daddy, like you always have. I remember you taking me onto your lap and trying to convince me that you were just standing in because there were so many new children that year, so Santa was too busy to visit everyone. What a whopper."

Meirah laughed then changed the subject. "Didn't you say you were going to see Sam today?"

"Yes, Mummy, I did. I've walked Oscar and Buttons and left them in the bungalow. If you get a minute, would you mind putting your nose in to check they're okay?"

"Of course, and I'll let them into the garden to stretch their legs. That way, if you want to stay a bit longer with Sam, they'll be all right."

CHAPTER TWENTY-SIX

Daisy gasped when she arrived at Sam's and saw the twins. "I can't believe how much they've grown in such a short time."

"Yes, and they're already showing different personalities. Niall says I'm imaging it, but he misses things when he's at work. You should see him with them. He's besotted."

"I'm not surprised. They're absolutely beautiful. How are you coping?"

"Neither of us is getting much sleep, as you may imagine. And I miss you being round the corner. How's everything going? Any news about Kirsty?"

"Nothing yet. She's still in a coma. It's been days now, and I don't think there's been any change at all."

"You'll let me know if you hear anything?"

"You know I will. Look, it's brightened up a bit. Are you up to taking my godchildren out and showing them to the world?"

"Definitely. I try to get out every day. I think it's good for them, and it's certainly good for me."

There was a small park nearby, not on the scale of Greenwich, but pretty and well cared for. Other young mothers were there with babies and toddlers, and Daisy found that Sam knew several of them already.

"I'm so pleased for you, Sam. Talk about the meaning of life! It's what you were made for."

"It is, isn't it? And to think I never knew until it happened. Have you got time to stay for lunch? There's quite a nice café in the park that stays open even at this time of the year. Only sandwiches and panini, but enough at this time of day."

"Will the babies be all right? What about their next feed?"

"We should be okay if we go now. Up for it?"

"You bet."

They were just finishing their coffee when Sam asked Daisy about the new enterprise.

"Things going well at Home Farm?"

"Smoothly so far. I'm waiting for something to go wrong, but it hasn't yet. And Buttons is adorable. I told you about her, didn't I?"

"Yes, and that you've got others coming straight after Christmas."

"For daycare, yes, and over the holidays for boarding as well. I can't believe my dream is coming true."

"And your other dream?" Sam asked gently.

"Don't go there, Sam. It is what it is, and I'll just have to live with it. I'm missing him dreadfully, but when he's here, it's like having my best friend with me — apologies to those present. I can bury the rest."

"Well, it's good to see you happy on one level, and no matter how sad the circumstances are, you're a lot better off than you were going through the motions with Jonathan."

"I can't believe I stayed with him for so long."

"At least he's got the chance to meet someone else now. As for you — a budding businesswoman! Who'd have thought?"

"It's amazing. I'm loving every minute of it."

The twins began to stir, so they bid a hasty retreat. Daisy left Sam at her door and headed back into Kent.

Daisy and Charlie had been talking every day for the past week, but there had been little discernible change to report. It therefore took her completely by surprise when, a few days later, she answered her phone to hear him say, "She's sitting up, Daisy. She's awake."

The relief was enormous. She'd expected the worst, though she hadn't admitted as much to Charlie.

"When? How?"

"Mid-afternoon, but I didn't call then because it was the middle of the night where you are."

"How is she?"

"Very weak, but apparently out of the woods. It should all be good from here on in."

"What happens next?"

"First of all, I'm taking Mum out for dinner to celebrate. Neither of us has eaten very much since we've been here. Cam wants to stay with Kirsty, and we thought we'd give them some time alone together. Daisy, I'm so excited I don't know what to do with myself. I didn't say anything to Mum, but for a while there I thought she wasn't going to make it."

Daisy didn't tell him about her own fears.

"How are things going at home? I haven't really taken in much of what you've said over the last few days."

"See, I knew you never listen to me," Daisy said, teasing now the worst was over. "We've had a quote for the clinic and several applications from vets. I've been to see Sam and the twins and they're beautiful. You're going to love Buttons. She as cute as, well, a button. Oh, and Oscar misses you."

"He told you that, of course."

"No, but he would if he could speak. I just know by the way he looks for you all the time. Oh, and Daddy was talking about getting his old Father Christmas outfit out of the loft. He hasn't worn it for years. I think he was just trying to cheer us all up."

"I shall look forward to seeing that. Do you hang stockings as well?"

"Of course we do. We're getting the tree today. Dad's already got the decorations down. That's what reminded him about dressing up. Apparently his costume is carefully wrapped and in a sealed bag. I think he's being a bit optimistic if he believes it'll still fit him."

"Well, if he can't get into it, maybe I can do the honours."

"You're coming home?"

"I hope so. There are still ten days to go. If Kirsty's recovery is as quick as they're suggesting, I'll just be in the way here. Mum's decided to stay, at least until the wedding. This disaster has knocked the stuffing out of her, and I don't think she wants to leave her little girl yet."

Daisy heart beat faster. She hadn't dared to believe she would see Charlie again so soon, but all she said was, "It'll be lovely to have you back."

"Will it snow, do you think? I'd love this to be my first white Christmas. It's so hot here you could fry an egg on the pavement."

"I can't promise you snow, Charlie, but I can say with a fair amount of certainty that it will be cold, very cold."

"Cold is good. Give my love to Meirah and Mike. I'll call again tomorrow."

"And give mine to everyone there. Bye."

Kirsty's progress was as rapid as the doctors had suggested it might be, and four days later they all flew from Cairns to Melbourne. Now back in her own home, the invalid was settled into a comfortable chair with her feet up and forbidden to do anything other than reach for the glass of water beside her. While Charlie sat with his sister, Cam popped into the office for a couple of hours and Gillian went off to do what she could to replenish the contents of the refrigerator.

"Would you like me to read you a story?" Charlie asked, the way he had when they were children.

He was only teasing, but Kirsty replied, "Yes, please, I'd like that."

By the time Gillian returned, three old favourites had been enjoyed and Kirsty was dozing peacefully.

"Expecting visitors?" asked Charlie as he helped his mother unpack the food.

"Of course not, but if there's something my daughter wants, I want to make sure it's here."

"If we knock down this wall and install some new cupboards, there might just be enough room," Charlie joked. It was a relief to them both to be able to enjoy the teasing now the danger had passed. "Do you fancy a sleeping bag on the floor, or would you like me to see about booking a couple of hotel rooms? I suddenly realised that with the old house being let, we have nowhere to stay."

"You may be young enough to sleep rough, Charlie, but I prefer a nice comfortable bed. Yes, please book something. I'm wondering if I can find a small apartment with a six-month let before Christmas. I don't want to be in a hotel over the holidays, and I don't want to be hanging around Kirsty and Cam's necks either."

"Don't worry, Mum. I'll get onto it for you. If there's anything suitable available, I'll run it by you."

"You do understand that I can't go back to England at the moment?"

"Of course. 'Give her my love and wish her better' isn't your style at all. Has James been in touch?"

"Once. Call me a cynic if you like, but it was coming up to the time his allowance was due for transfer. I couldn't help thinking he was making sure I didn't renege on our agreement."

"I don't think you're a cynic at all. A realist, maybe. Let's just be grateful that both James's daughters take after their mothers."

"How is Daisy and the business? I forgot to ask today, what with all the rushing around."

"It's going really well. She's already got customers and we're barely officially open. If it carries on at this rate, we might even begin to turn a profit by this time next year."

"You're really excited about this project, aren't you?"

"Well, for starters I can't believe how much I love having dogs around. Don't repeat that to Kirsty. She's never going to forgive me in any case. Also, and I'm sure you'll understand this, I always loved working with you…" He hesitated. "But that was your business. You started it and much as I was involved, it was never my project. With this, I'm starting fresh. It will be up to me and Daisy if it succeeds or fails, but I have to try."

"And does Daisy know how you feel about her?" Gillian asked gently.

"No, Mum, and she's never going to. I'm lucky to have her at all. Her terms are better than no terms. If it's a brother she wants, I'll always be there for her."

In the end Charlie didn't make it back until Christmas Eve. He got a taxi from the airport and arrived to find Home Farm shrouded in white. There was a hush about the place he'd never experienced before. Daisy was busy in the kennels. Billy, Stephanie Webb's dog, had started his week's board two days earlier. He'd welcomed Daisy like the long-lost friend she was and lost no time in bonding with Buttons, who was still attached to Daisy's heel.

Charlie hauled Daisy to her feet, and if the hug they exchanged was somewhat desperate on both sides they were able to put it down to their relief about Kirsty.

"It's magical. Like some of the cards we had back in Oz and could never relate to in the middle of an Australian summer. Your parents' house looks unbelievably beautiful. And look at this!" Charlie took in the final details that had been added since he'd last been there. "You've worked miracles."

"No, it's just that now there are dogs in here it feels more real. I'm really impressed with the builders as well. The inside areas are draught-free, even though there's access to the outside runs. They've done a fantastic job. Have you seen Mum and Dad?"

"Not yet. I thought I'd find you in here, so this is where I came first. Where's Oscar, and who's this?" he asked, looking down at the little dog who was tugging at his trouser leg to get his attention.

"Where are your manners, young lady? This is Buttons. She demands attention but, and don't tell her I said this, she's absolutely adorable."

"Until she learns English, I think we're fairly safe."

"Oscar's back at the bungalow. He's had a walk, played in the snow and decided it's time for his beauty sleep. Do you want to see him first or my parents?"

Charlie hesitated and she grinned.

"I won't tell them you had to think about it. Come on over to the house. They'll be delighted to see you."

With a lightness in their step that both had been lacking for a while, they made their way to the farmhouse kitchen, where Mike was already making preparations for tomorrow's great feast. Even Meirah was helping.

Mike and Charlie clapped each other on the back and Meirah was swept off her feet and swung around the room.

"For a man who's just travelled halfway across the world, you're remarkably fresh," she said.

"It's the relief, Meirah," he said. "It's hard to believe how ill Kirsty was. By the time I left, she was home and she'd spent some time sitting in the sun, so she'd lost that pasty look. Cam didn't bother to go back to work so close to Christmas. Between him and Mum, she's being pretty much spoiled."

"We're all delighted she's made such a good recovery, and to have you back again. I believe you're going to act as stand-in this year."

For a moment Charlie looked puzzled, then he looked at Mike and smiled. "Couldn't squeeze yourself into the Father Christmas outfit, eh? I'd be delighted to do the honours."

Daisy took Charlie into the living room to inspect the tree, which was really quite splendid, then they went across to the bungalow to be reunited with Oscar. Daisy said that his excited barking could probably be heard on the other side of the county.

"So where are we up to with the vet?" Charlie asked later that evening. "I'm sorry, Daisy — there's been so much going on I can't remember what you and Mike decided. Employ or rent?"

"Rent. We've made a huge investment in the building — did I tell you they're starting to equip the surgery straight after the holidays? — but that should reap its own rewards. Other than as landlords, we won't be involved, which will help ease our admin burden. We should gain huge benefits, though, when the practice is established. Not just for boarding and daycare, but for the grooming parlour as well. I even wondered about stocking feed, but there's so much variety, and with so many dogs needing special diets I decided it wasn't really viable, not with all the other outlets that stock pet supplies."

"You've taken to this like the proverbial duck to water, haven't you? Did you know you had a business head on you before all this began?"

"I didn't know I had one now. Thank you, I take that as a compliment, particularly from you. Anyway, Daddy and I did the interviewing together and there was one obvious choice for us both. The lease is being drawn up and she should begin on the first of February."

"Another woman! It's lucky Mike's here or I'd be well and truly outnumbered."

"You'll like her. She qualified six years ago and she's been with the same group ever since. She's moving now because she's split with her boyfriend and wants to be closer to her family in Maidstone. It was a mainly small animal practice, so she's had plenty of experience in the right area. Her name's Belinda."

CHAPTER TWENTY-SEVEN

Daisy and Charlie were walking the dogs on Christmas Day morning, having been ordered out of the way at the big house. There was some attempt at making a snowman, but as Oscar thought nothing was greater fun than running straight through the middle they gave it up fairly quickly. They went back to the kennels, rubbed down the dogs and fed the boarders, much to Oscar's indignation. Charlie scratched behind his ear.

"It's okay, old chap. You'll get yours as soon as we get home."

It had taken no time at all for Oscar's affections to be re-engaged.

"Look at you," Daisy said. "You're besotted."

"He's just pleased to see me, that's all."

"Not him, Charlie, you!"

Charlie tried to put a snowball down Daisy's neck, but she was too quick for him. When Oscar had eaten and was curled up in his basket, they went to their respective rooms to change for lunch.

Daisy had put on something special. She still wore trousers, but they were beautifully cut. She took her rather expensive long black boots with her, last year's Christmas present from her parents, carrying them across to the main house while wearing her wellies. Her emerald-coloured top clung to her, setting off her curves to good effect, and a simple chain with a drop pendant added a touch of class. When she changed her footwear, the outfit was complete. Charlie thought she looked stunning.

"What is that amazing smell?" Charlie asked as he crossed the threshold of the main house.

"I never ask," said Daisy. "I just wait to see what's put in front of me. I've never been disappointed yet, and I don't see why this year should be any different."

At some point since he'd arrived back in Kent, Charlie had managed to creep unnoticed into the living room and deposit two small parcels under the tree, one for Daisy and the other for Meirah and Mike. It was family tradition to open their presents before lunch. Charlie was delighted to see that, next to all the stockings hanging from the great mantelpiece, there was one for Oscar.

"Shall I go and get him?" he asked.

"I think perhaps we'll leave him until after we've eaten, Charlie, but I promise you can be the one to give him his presents," said Daisy.

"Is there a squeaky toy there, Daisy?"

"That's for me to know and you to find out."

Meirah opened her present. "Brilliant, Charlie. This is perfect. I'll be able to go as often as I like, and if Mike doesn't want to come with me I'll take you instead."

"What? What is it?" Daisy asked, craning her neck to see.

"A year's membership to the Royal Academy. I won't have to miss anything now."

For a moment Charlie looked a bit crestfallen. "Not your thing, Mike?"

"Oh yes, and I'm as pleased as Meirah is. It's just that I don't choose to go to absolutely everything they put on there."

"Can I open mine now?" Daisy interrupted.

"Yes. Just don't ask me to change it. It's a long way back to Australia."

Daisy gasped when she opened the small box, because the Aboriginal necklace inside was stunning. It was made of shells, dried fruit, beads and seeds, and painted with an assortment of bright colours. And it screamed joy.

"It's lovely, Charlie. Thank you." She put it on straight away. "We haven't got you anything nearly as grand."

"I wasn't expecting anything at all. I wasn't even sure I'd be here."

This reminded them all that they hadn't phoned Gillian yet, and it was now quite late in Australia. Charlie sent a text asking if she was still awake. His phone rang immediately.

"Of course I'm awake," said Gillian when he answered. "It's Christmas, isn't it? How are you all?"

"We're good. And how's my baby sister?"

"I left her and Cam about an hour ago. She still gets tired quickly, but apart from that she's absolutely fine."

"Everyone here wishes you a great holiday. Take care and I'll talk to you soon."

"You don't get rid of me that easily. Let me talk to Meirah."

"She wants to talk to you," he said, passing her the phone.

The two women chatted for a couple of minutes before Meirah handed it back.

"What a mad world. They had their Christmas dinner on the beach. A barbecue, of all things!"

"I'll take a photo tomorrow and send it to her. She'll be as delighted as I was to see all this snow."

Daisy had bought Charlie a cloth cap, a country squire type, more as a joke than anything else, but actually it quite suited him. The sweater with reinforced elbow patches from her parents went down well too.

"I see you're all determined I'm going to become an English gentleman."

"No, Charlie, they're working men's clothes. I wouldn't be without mine in the winter," said Mike.

Daisy's present from her parents was a spa day for two, which she declared she would share with Sam when the babies were old enough to leave with Niall, and Meirah was thrilled with the new brushes Daisy had bought her. Mike's Mr Happy apron was donned immediately and suited him perfectly.

"That's my cue. Okay, everyone, let's go and sit at the table. It's time to eat."

It was dark by the time they'd finished eating. They'd have stayed much longer, but Daisy said she needed to go and check up on the residents in the block.

"I'll go home first and change into something more suitable."

"Hang on, I'll join you," said Charlie.

"Why don't you both come back later? We can have a brandy and I'll do something with the leftovers, if anyone has room," said Meirah.

"I didn't know you cooked, Meirah," said Charlie.

"I don't do it very often. Anyway, this isn't cooking. This is doing artistic things with the already-cooked. A subtle difference, which I'm sure you can appreciate."

Daisy and Charlie crunched through the snow towards the bungalow.

"Gosh, we must have been hungry. In the rush to get over to the big house, we left the gate open." Daisy's smile turned to shock when she saw the front door too was ajar.

"Oscar! OSCAR!" Charlie yelled.

But he wasn't there.

It had been snowing steadily all afternoon, and there was that beautiful glow about the place. Neither Daisy nor Charlie were in the mood to enjoy it.

"Look, Charlie, you can just about see some tracks here. At least he hasn't gone towards the road."

"Go on then. I'll just get a couple of torches and follow you. Have you got your phone, in case we need to separate?"

"Yes!" she called over her shoulder. She was already on her way. Charlie caught up with her fairly quickly. Oscar's tracks were quite faint, but different enough from the rest of the terrain for them to follow, until they got to the stream. There was no continuing track on the other side.

"What shall we do? Split up, do you think?"

"We stand more chance of finding him quickly if we do. We'll give it ten minutes and then check in."

"And then what, Charlie? Give up?"

"Of course not. We'll give it another ten, then another until we find him."

Both found it hard going. There was no discernible footpath. Daisy stumbled more than once, and Charlie was whipped in the face several times by overhanging branches.

Daisy checked in at the agreed time, though she knew Charlie would have let her know immediately if he'd found anything.

"No. I'm going on. The stream's getting a bit wider here and there are several small boulders. Daisy, what if he's got out the other side? We could have gone straight past him without noticing. I keep flashing my torch over there, but I doubt I'd have seen anything even if he was there."

"We just have to keep trying, Charlie. I'll talk to you again soon."

The next call was no more productive than the previous one, but five minutes later Daisy's phone rang.

"I've found him, but hurry, Daisy. I'm really worried."

She had no recollection later of her headlong flight along the river, but there were many scratches and bruises that were evidence of her panic. She found Charlie in the process of lifting Oscar and carrying him back across the stream to the home side.

"His paw was caught between the boulders. He couldn't move. He was just lying there, Daisy."

Tears were streaming down his face. Oscar was seemingly lifeless in his arms. Daisy turned her attention to the dog.

"He's cold and barely conscious, but there's a definitely heartbeat. Thank goodness he's got a big coat. None of the little ones would have survived this long."

They were running, or at least attempting to. Oscar was heavy, even for someone the size of Charlie. They went straight to the big house where they knew the fire would still be roaring away and laid him on the hearth.

"Towels. Lots of them."

Mike ran off at Daisy's request. He and Meirah were both shocked. The last they knew, Daisy and Charlie had gone to check up on the boarders.

Coffee was made to warm the very cold humans while they rubbed and cajoled in an effort to bring Oscar back to life.

"Should we take him to the vet?"

"Christmas Day, Charlie? I don't think so. In any case, the best thing we can do for him now is to bring his temperature up."

"He looks as bad as he did after the fire. They weren't sure he was going to make it then either."

"He's going to be all right," Daisy said with conviction.

After what seemed an eternity, they were rewarded by a flickering of his eye and a slight movement of his head.

"You'll want to stay with him," said Mike. "Would you like me to go over and see how the others are getting on?"

"That would be great, Dad. Their feeds are all ready, up on the shelf and labelled. You might need to pick up any poo, but otherwise they should be okay. Oh, and could you just check their water as well, please?"

Slowly Oscar came back to them. The trembling that had wracked his body ceased, and he showed some signs of interest in his surroundings. Daisy examined his paw.

"Doesn't look too bad. He must have had the sense at least not to struggle when it got caught. How on earth did you get it out without hurting him?"

"I honestly don't know, Daisy, but at that moment I could have moved mountains."

Hours later they were all sitting round the fire, doing minimal justice to Meirah's culinary efforts. The brandy was doing its job, though. Oscar, absolutely exhausted from his ordeal, was content to lie in his family circle.

"I've just remembered — he hasn't had his stocking yet."

"Okay, Charlie, go on then."

Charlie took it down from the mantelpiece and spread the contents in front of Oscar. He ignored the doggy treats but picked up the new toy in his jaw and squeezed. It squeaked. It was as if he was saying thank you. He laid his head down again. Daisy smiled.

"You're welcome."

CHAPTER TWENTY-EIGHT

The next day, Charlie phoned Kirsty. "Did you get my photo of the snow?" he asked. "Isn't it amazing?"

"I wouldn't mind a bit of that right now, Charlie. It's as hot as Hell's kitchen here. There's a risk of fires."

"It's a mad world we live in, isn't it? Mum and Cam okay?"

"They're fine. We had friends for a barbecue this evening. He's just clearing up. He's still treating me like an invalid and won't let me lift a finger."

"Enjoy it while you can."

"I will, don't you worry. Mum's not coming around too much. At first I thought it was because she didn't want to be in the way, but I really think she's enjoying her new-found freedom. No work and she's off to Bondi with all the other holidaymakers."

"Good on her."

"So, are you all having a good Christmas there?" Kirsty asked.

"It's been mixed."

"How do you mean?"

"We had a bit of an incident with Oscar yesterday." Charlie went on to tell Kirsty what had happened, ending with, "I'm here with him now. He's much better, but it'll take him a couple of days to recover fully. It's a public holiday here today, but we're going to take him to the vet tomorrow, just to get him checked over."

"Seems like a good idea. Give him a big hug for me."

"I will. Talk soon. Love you."

"You too. Bye."

As it turned out, Oscar was so obviously fine they didn't take him to the vet, even for his paw, which was just a little bruised. What they did do was attach mechanical closers to the door and the gate so the same thing wouldn't happen again, repeating the exercise over at the kennels. The snow stopped as quickly as it had begun, and by New Year's Eve the roads were clear enough for Daisy and Charlie to drive to Sam and Niall's, where they'd been invited for a party.

"You're a brave man, taking this on with two babies," Charlie said to Niall when they arrived.

"We're not getting any sleep anyway, Charlie, so if we're up we may as well be enjoying ourselves."

There were maybe twenty people in the flat, comfortable rather than cramped, and Daisy caught up with some old friends she hadn't seen for some time. Sam disappeared for a while to feed the twins, dragging Daisy with her. There was an unmistakable glow about her as she fed first one and then the other. Daisy was pressed into holding little Daisy while her brother suckled so enthusiastically that his godmother was moved to say, "Hey, leave some for your sister."

"Don't worry, there's plenty there. It's amazing how the body compensates. What should be the right amount for one becomes enough for two. Next time you come, they'll be partly on the bottle, so you'll be able to help me."

The thought filled Daisy with wonder and fear at the same time.

"I'd be terrified."

"Nah, you'll be a natural."

Sam could have no idea of the impact the conversation was having on her friend. Daisy had given up all thoughts of having children of her own, but something changed that night. She began to wonder if there was anybody out there she could love enough to have children with.

They carried the babies, one each, into the living room. Midnight was fast approaching, and Sam wanted them to be in the midst of everything when they all heralded the New Year. Daisy glanced quickly at Charlie. He couldn't know that in her heart she was saying goodbye. It was with little hope of her future happiness that she raised her glass in a toast.

Something changed for Charlie too that evening. It had been a while since he'd met anyone new. There were a couple of very attractive young women at the party, and conversations that had begun out of good manners became more personal. He realised he'd missed socialising, that if he couldn't have Daisy there was still a world outside. They hardly saw each other the whole evening, and while he was aware all the time of where she was, he was still able to give his full attention to his companion. No-one was more astonished than him when he accepted an invitation to go to the theatre the following Saturday.

"I've had the tickets for ages," said his new acquaintance, Rebecca. "A friend was supposed to be coming with me, but she took a last-minute holiday. The play's supposed to be really good. Would you like to come?"

"Only if I can take you out to dinner first."

And that was it. Charlie had a date with Rebecca, and Daisy had decided to turn her life around. It was two very different people who drove back to Kent when the party was over.

A few days later work began on the new veterinary clinic, and at the weekend Charlie went on his date with Rebecca.

"Are you okay with this, kitten?" Mike asked Daisy.

"Yes, Daddy, as it happens I am. These last nine months or so have been a whirlwind, but I made a resolution last week."

"Do you want to share it with me?"

"I'm loving the work here and I love being back at Home Farm, but there's a whole world out there that I've hardly touched. I feel comfortable with Charlie and I hope that never changes, but I don't want to spend the rest of my life being someone's sister. I'm going out to meet people."

"People?"

"Specifically men. I want what you and Mummy have had all these years."

"And children?"

"Yes, I want children. I didn't even know it before, but when I saw the twins last week, it was as if lightning had flashed."

Mike returned to the beginning of the conversation. "So you're okay with Charlie seeing other women?"

"I won't say it doesn't hurt, but I have to be, don't I?"

"Then I'm right behind you. It's all very well burying yourself in work, particularly when it's work you enjoy, but you're right, there's more to life than that."

"It's a new year, Daddy, and a new Daisy. I'm going to do something. In the meantime, I'd better check that the kennels are secure for the night. In a way it's good we don't have any boarders at the moment. The noise the workmen are making during the day would be enough to spook even the most-well-adjusted dog. I'm not worried that we don't have any bookings at the moment either. We have some daycare, which I think will grow quicker than anything else, and now that Christmas is over most people won't be going away until Easter."

"I'll walk over to the kennels with you if you like."

"Great."

"By the way, your mother has no idea how you feel about Charlie. She said quite innocently that it was good to see Charlie going out and enjoying himself."

Daisy wished she felt it was good, but at least she was trying.

Charlie also had mixed feelings about his situation. Rebecca was a good companion, easy to be with, and their dinner had been relaxed with no undercurrent of expectation on either side. What had thrown him was the theatre. Having no idea what they were going to see, he was taken back several months to the day he'd been there with Gillian and Kirsty. That naturally made him think about Daisy.

While Charlie promised to phone Rebecca, each knew it was probably a one-off date, enjoyable while it lasted. He drove back to Home Farm, still using the car Gillian had hired, happy to be out there again and determined to continue on this path. How he was going to meet people as a stranger in town, he didn't know. Ask Daisy? No, she didn't seem to have a vast circle of friends, and if she introduced him to them he would probably have to see more of her than was good for his peace of mind. It was hard enough working with her every day without revealing his true feelings. It seemed to him that Niall would be his best route. They got on well, and he was fairly sure he would be welcome on the monthly boys' night out.

Daisy was asleep when he got back. She'd left the outside light on for him, and when Oscar greeted him with loud barks he shushed him and closed the kitchen door on them both. There was a half empty bottle of wine on the worktop with a single glass. He was tempted to take another and put his feet up in front of the television, but it had been a long evening. He went to bed. If Oscar's barking had disturbed Daisy, she showed no sign of it.

The next day, Daisy's phone rang. It was an unknown caller. Curious, she answered.

"Daisy? Is that you?"

"Yes, it's me. Who's that?"

"Jason."

"Jason?"

"I met you at Sam and Niall's party. I'm the one with the bu…"

"Bubbly hair! Yes, of course."

They both laughed as they'd laughed then at his mop, not as long as hers but the same colour and with the same curls.

"I hope you don't mind me phoning. Niall gave me your number."

"Of course I don't."

"You see, when I saw you holding the baby well, naturally, I thought it was yours. I don't know them very well — Niall's a workmate — and I had no idea they had twins."

Daisy could see where this was leading and felt a little stir of interest.

"Anyway, I was talking to Niall and he explained, so I asked him if you had a partner and he said he didn't think so."

"He's right. I don't."

"Good. Well, not good of course, but good for me. I hope."

Daisy smiled. It seemed Jason's personality was as outrageous as his hair. She waited.

"So, I was wondering if maybe we could see each other. Dinner, maybe?"

"I'd love to. Did you have anything particular in mind?"

"I don't even know where you live."

"West Kent."

"Oh! I'm across the river in Essex. We could wave at each other. I'm pretty close to the bridge, though. Do you think lunch would be a better idea, just until we get our bearings?"

Just until we get our bearings? He's obviously looking beyond a first date, Daisy thought.

"Yes, I think it's a great idea, particularly at this time of year." She felt it was probably her turn to make some kind of contribution. "Can you do this Sunday? There are two or three places fairly nearby, if you don't mind venturing south."

"No problem. I look forward to getting to know you better now I know you're not nursing a baby."

CHAPTER TWENTY-NINE

On Sunday, Jason arrived at Home Farm for his date with Daisy.

"Wow, this place is beautiful," he said. "Have you lived here for long?"

"Most of my life, except for four years in the middle and a bit at the beginning that I don't remember. My parents moved here when I was very little."

They were standing in the drive and Daisy pointed to the bungalow.

"That's where I live now. With Charlie, my brother."

"Yes, I remember meeting him at the party. Talk of the devil," he said as Charlie came out from the kennels. "Hello, Charlie. We met at Sam and Niall's on New Year's Eve. I'm Jason."

"Yes, I remember you of course."

The men shook hands and Jason looked down at Oscar, glued to Charlie's heel but peering up at him with interest.

"And you are?" Jason asked, extending his hand again. Oscar obligingly raised his paw. "He's a great guy. What do you call him?"

"'Menace' some of the time, but his name's Oscar."

"Chewed socks?"

"Ah. I see you know dogs."

"Gotta love 'em, though, haven't you?"

"We wouldn't be doing what we are if not."

"What do you do?"

Daisy was amused to see the two of them becoming engrossed in dog talk.

"Come and see the kennel block," said Charlie. "We're very proud of it." He hauled Jason away. So Jason was a dog lover. Always a good point in her book.

"I'll be in the bungalow when you're ready," she called after him.

Thinking she had time for a quick shower after spending the early part of the day cleaning the kennels, she walked into the living room with one towel wrapped around her head and another around her body just as the two men came in.

"And I thought we were going out for lunch," Jason teased. "On our first date too. I didn't take you for that kind of a girl, Daisy."

She squeaked and retreated. "With you in a minute," she called from the bedroom. "Talk amongst yourselves."

"You obviously get on really well," said Jason as he and Daisy drove to their chosen restaurant. "It's not always that way with brothers and sisters."

"We have a shared passion."

"You don't look a bit alike. He certainly doesn't have the outrageous hair."

"Look who's talking! No, we have different mothers. I get the curls from mine."

"I presume that would account for the Aussie accent. It's pretty strong."

"Yes, he's only been in this country for, what, just under a year. His mother and sister came for a while but they've gone home now. Charlie decided to stay."

"And your father?"

"Out of the picture. He left when I was tiny. Mike's the only father I've ever known. I hope you'll meet him later. And Mum. Take a left here and then the first right."

"Is that the place, down there just before the bend?"

"Yes, that's it. It's a favourite of mine, but I haven't been here for ages. I hope you like it."

"I'm sure it's going to become a favourite of mine too," Jason said warmly.

Three hours later, they'd finished their meal and Jason sat back contentedly. "I can see why you like it here. That was brilliant. You said there were two or three places like this?"

"Yes."

"Want to try one of the others next week?"

"You don't waste any time, do you?"

"Daisy, I've sat here with you for nearly three hours. I haven't once looked at my watch. We haven't stopped talking. The face opposite me is beautiful." She blushed. "Yeah, sure I want to do it again."

"Then I'd love to. But now I ought to be getting back."

"Didn't you say you've no boarders at the moment? What's to do?"

"You know what, you're right. It's just that like I told you, Charlie deals with the finance and the business side of things. It's my job to make sure everything goes smoothly on the ground, so I guess I'm feeling the pressure to be there. Once we're up and running properly, I'm hoping in a perverse sort of way that my time won't be my own. But that hasn't happened yet. I quite like this me time."

"I'll take that as a compliment. Next Sunday, then?"

"I'd love to."

Mike's car pulled into the drive just ahead of them and Daisy introduced him to Jason.

"Come in, young man, come in," said Mike. "Beer? Coffee?"

"Coffee would be lovely. I'm already intoxicated by your daughter's company, and I still have to drive home."

It might have sounded smarmy coming from someone else, but Jason was so obviously genuine it seemed a perfectly natural thing to say.

Meirah breezed through into the kitchen to get some orange juice and rushed out again to get back to her latest creation. She was paint-splattered and dishevelled as ever, and Jason gave Daisy a smile of pure delight.

"She's adorable," he said as he stood by his car, saying goodbye. "I can see exactly what you're going to be like in thirty years or so, except maybe without the paint."

He kissed Daisy on the tip of her nose and left. She was glad he hadn't attempted anything more, while at the same time feeling a little disappointed. She realised she hadn't been kissed in a long time. Daisy watched the tail lights of his car until they disappeared round the bend.

By the end of the week the veterinary surgery was finished, they had two more dogs booked in for daycare and two boarders until the end of the month. Daisy worried about leaving them at night in such a vast place, though their own units were self-contained, but her practical side told her they'd have been alone in their own homes anyway, assuming they didn't sleep at the end of their owners' beds. She would walk them morning and afternoon and put them next to each other for company.

Realising how busy she suddenly was, Daisy rang Jason. "Jason, it's Daisy. It's about tomorrow."

"Something wrong?"

"Not wrong, exactly. It's just that Belinda's starting on Monday. You know, the new vet I told you about. She's coming tomorrow at twelve to meet Charlie and look around the place now that it's finished."

"And you need to be there."

"I knew you'd understand."

"Why don't I come anyway? It can't take all day. If we don't manage lunch, we can have tea. If not, I can always hold your mother's brushes for her."

"You're not cross?"

"Of course I'm not cross."

"I'll see you tomorrow then. If you're already in the surgery when I get there, I'll go and talk to Oscar."

"Great. Just knock at the big house. Dad will let you into the bungalow."

The next day, Belinda was standing in the middle of the surgery, turning in a circle as she tried to take everything in.

"What a great place! I'm amazed at the attention to detail," she said.

"The contractors were fantastic people to work with. They've obviously done it many times before. When you employ specialists, you get what you want. They were meticulous about including the things you asked for."

"Thank you, Charlie. It's like Christmas all over again. I've already made lists of everything I need. Tomorrow I'll start ordering. The suppliers are usually pretty quick with deliveries. Oh, and I'll be looking for a nurse. Perhaps you can tell me about the local press, though I've already placed an ad in two vet magazines and had some email replies. I haven't checked the addresses yet, which is why it might be a good idea to advertise locally as well. Sorry, I'm babbling."

"It's great to see you so excited. Daisy and I feel exactly the same, don't we, Daisy?"

"Excited! That's an understatement. Ever since building began, there's been a current rolling around in my head. I either sleep like a baby from exhaustion or spend half the night worrying in case something's been forgotten."

"Me too, and the more you try to relax, the worse it is. I keep seeing lists."

"Is there anything else you need to see, Belinda?" asked Charlie.

"No, I think that's it, Charlie. Thank you. I'll see you tomorrow morning then."

"What are you going to do now?"

"I'm going back to my parents' place. It's a bit of a commute, but I'll find somewhere closer when I've got time to look."

"Why don't you join us for lunch? I'm going out with my boyfriend." It sounded odd in Daisy's ears and even more so in Charlie's. "I'm sure he won't mind if you both come with."

The words were out before she could stop them. She hoped she was right about Jason not minding.

Charlie smiled. "Well, we all have to eat, don't we? Is that okay with you, Belinda?"

"Yes, I'd love to, Charlie, and I'd love to meet your boyfriend."

"Great. Charlie, why don't you phone The Herring Gull and see if they can change the booking from two to four. It gets pretty busy just about everywhere around here on Sunday lunchtime. I'll go up to the bungalow and tell Jason. He should be here by now."

If Jason was disappointed, he certainly didn't allow it to show. He even offered to drive.

"That way, you can have a couple of drinks to welcome Belinda."

The Herring Gull was every bit as good as the place they'd been to the previous week, and it was half past four before they all realised the place was empty except for them and the staff were beginning to hover.

"What a great lunch," said Jason when he'd driven them all back to Home Farm. "I can hardly move. I won't come in. Lovely meeting you, Belinda, and seeing you again, Charlie." He turned to Daisy, sitting next to him. "I'll call you. Take care." He leaned over and kissed her nose again before she and the others got out of the car.

Daisy got on well with Belinda straight away. So did Charlie. Every time she saw them together, Daisy was convinced he was trying to make a good impression.

Ah well, I guess it had to happen sometime, she thought. *I could have done without it being in our own front yard, though.*

It was true that Charlie was attracted to Belinda. Not having yet made contact with Niall, he thought there might be the possibility of doing this thing on his own. Normally he wouldn't have dreamed of mixing business with pleasure, but in theory Belinda's veterinary clinic was a completely separate entity.

"Need any help emptying those boxes? I can be your shelf filler if it's useful," he offered one morning while Daisy was out walking the boarders.

"Actually, that would help immensely. I know where everything is supposed to go. I've labelled the shelves already, but it'll be much quicker if I hand them to you straight from the box and you stack them. Not that I'm pushed for time. It'll be a while before I have any patients, I guess."

"Are you worried?"

"At the moment, I don't want to be stealing other vets' customers. I would expect people to have a certain amount of allegiance to their existing surgery. What I am hoping to do is pick up the small animal breeds locally, as it's quite a way to the nearest practice. But you know that already, of course. In the meantime, I've enough backup to carry me for a while."

"You'd be astonished at how quickly word gets around. I know it doesn't seem like much, but we didn't expect to have any business at all for a while yet."

They worked in silence for a while, with Belinda occasionally telling Charlie where things were to go when he couldn't find the right label.

"Do you have to rush off this evening?" he asked. "Would you like to go for a drink?"

"As it happens, I have an appointment to view a small flat. Another time would be lovely, though."

It didn't feel like a rebuff, but Charlie didn't push it. He'd try again later.

By the end of that week, Belinda had found a furnished flat with a short-term lease that would be ideal for the time being. It was vacant, so she moved on Sunday.

"No time like the present," she said to Charlie, ringing him from her new home. "Once the money was transferred, the landlord was happy for me to move in straight away."

"Do you need any help with anything?" he asked.

"Not really, thanks, but I wouldn't mind afterwards going for that drink you offered me the other day."

"In that case, call me when you're ready and I'll come and get you."

"Thank you, Charlie. I'll look forward to it."

He spent the day working on his laptop while Daisy and Jason sampled yet another of the culinary delights on offer in the area.

"No Belinda and Charlie today?" Jason asked when he turned up at Home Farm.

Daisy explained about Belinda's move. "Why don't I drive today, Jason? You've come all the way over here and you've got to get back as well."

"Suits me. Is it a long way?"

"Well, we haven't quite exhausted everything in this area. It'll be nice later in the year to explore a bit further afield, but in this weather it's not so much fun, particularly when you've already driven so far."

They were completely at ease in each other's company, but Daisy felt there was something missing. It wasn't just the kisses on the nose, pleasurable though they were. It was almost like a role reversal between Jason and Charlie. When she was with Jason, with whom she'd love to have felt a sexual tug, it was almost as if they were brother and sister. With Charlie, whom she fancied desperately, it didn't feel like he was her brother at all. She wondered how Jason felt. She could hardly ask him, not yet anyway.

As she got home, Charlie went out. She went up to the big house to see her parents.

"You mother's in her studio for a change," Mike joked. "Anything wrong, kitten? You look troubled."

"Not wrong, exactly."

"Jason?"

"Yes. I like him, I really do."

"But Charlie's getting in the way."

"I don't think it's that particularly. Even if there was no Charlie, I think I'd feel like this anyway. It's almost like being with Sam, except he's a man. I'm really comfortable with him, but there's no spark."

"Does he know?"

"I get the feeling it's the same for him. He hasn't even kissed me yet."

"Hmm. I see what you mean."

"He wants to go out again next Sunday. He asked if Charlie and Belinda might like to join us. You don't do that if you're emotionally involved with someone, do you? Not at this stage anyway."

"Do you think it's time to let it go?"

"Not really. Not if he feels the same and he's enjoying it too. It's fun. I'd just like to get a feel for the ground I'm standing on."

"Why don't you ask him?"

"I think I have to."

CHAPTER THIRTY

"This is really nice, Belinda," said Charlie when he'd arrived at her flat. "I'm not surprised you snapped it up."

"I think it's been used as a holiday let up till now."

"Anything I can do here, or are you ready to go?"

"Going would be good. I'll have to do some shopping tomorrow. The one thing I didn't think of was to bring any food."

"Ah, shall we have dinner then?"

"I do like a man who's quick on the uptake. Yes, Charlie, dinner would be lovely. I'm starving."

Though they didn't know it, they went to the same place that evening as Daisy and Jason had been at lunchtime.

"There seems to be an ample supply of pub restaurants around here. It's been several weeks and I haven't yet been to the same one twice," Charlie said once they'd finished their meal.

"It sounds as if you're making a hobby of it."

"Not quite, and of course I was back in Oz for a while."

"Yes, I heard. Your sister. Can you tell me about it?"

He summarised what had happened.

"Sounds like a nightmare."

"It was, Belinda. We really thought we were going to lose her."

There was a pause while they tried to re-establish their previously light mood. Belinda pushed her chair back from the table.

"That was lovely, Charlie, but it's getting late. I think we should go."

He dropped her at her flat and went home. It had been a nice evening and he was pretty sure she'd enjoyed it too, but there was something missing. He was almost ashamed of the thought. Daisy was missing.

Belinda interviewed and employed a nurse the following Tuesday and had her first patient the next day. It was Buttons. She'd cut one of her pads, and rather than take any chances Daisy had taken her straight across to the clinic. A shameless attention-seeker, Buttons was happy to be examined and treated. While she was there, Daisy took the opportunity to ask about Sunday lunch.

"Jason and I were wondering if you and Charlie would like to join us again. It was so nice that first time."

"Well, I can't speak for Charlie, but I'd love to," Belinda replied.

"Wonderful, and as you're so local now we'll pick you up."

When she put the same question to Charlie, he hesitated almost imperceptibly before saying, "Yes, that would be great."

Daisy had no idea what to make of it. Were Belinda and Charlie seeing each other or not?

Things were progressing quite nicely at Home Farm, and though boarding was sporadic the daycare side had really taken off. With the kennels unoccupied, Daisy used them as a holding post for some of her charges when it became easier to walk them in small groups rather than all together. Three walks in the morning and three in the afternoon left her positively glowing with health.

Her relationship with Jason wasn't making nearly as much progress, but for the time being it suited her. She hadn't yet summoned up the courage to ask him where she stood. It had never been the right time or the appropriate thing to do. They'd slipped into a routine with which both seemed content. Jason phoned her once during the week, usually on a Wednesday evening, and Sunday lunchtimes continued as before, except sometimes Daisy would do the cooking instead of them going out. Belinda and Charlie joined them once or twice and on one occasion Daisy drove into Essex, but as she kept looking at her watch and worrying, the experiment wasn't repeated.

Belinda's side of things was also taking off nicely too. As well as the usual cats and dogs, she saw a variety of smaller creatures — rabbits, guinea pigs, mice. There was one untreatable fracture where amputation wasn't an option, and she had to put the animal to sleep. Otherwise there was no drama, until one day a very worried little girl came in with her mother.

"It's Casey. She been asleep for such a long time. Almost since I first got her. Is she dead?" the girl asked in that straightforward way children had.

Belinda looked in the box. Amongst several layers of warm packing, she found a tortoise. "Casey?"

"'Cos she's got her own luggage on her back."

"Ah, of course. Well, I think I can promise you Casey is going to be fine. You know how cold it's been. Tortoises don't like the cold, so instead of feeling it as we do they just go to sleep for a very long time until it's all over and spring comes around again. You've wrapped Casey up very well, and I think the best thing you can do for her is leave her as she is. In a few weeks, you could take a look at her from time to time to see if she's started to wake up. She'll let you know when she's ready."

"You're sure?"

"I'm sure, but if you're worried you can come and see me any time."

Daisy had been lucky enough to witness this exchange. Belinda's nurse had the afternoon off and she'd been invited to stand in.

"That was lovely. You could see how worried she was and how much better she felt afterwards. It was great you took so much time to explain things to her," said Daisy.

"Well, I expect Casey is as precious to her as Oscar is to you. My first pet was the centre of my world, and I remember how worried I was about her."

"What was she?"

"A rat."

"What!"

"Didn't you know, Daisy? Domestic rats make the most wonderful pets, and they're very intelligent."

"I didn't actually, no."

They soon had another new inmate, a cat who had wandered in without a microchip or a collar and for whom, try as they might, they couldn't identify an owner.

"Well, if she's here to stay, we'd better give her a name. I quite like having a cat in the surgery. There was one where I worked before. Any ideas about what to call her?"

"It's you she's chosen, Belinda, so it's up to you."

"How about Bump?"

"Bump?"

"Haven't you seen it yet? Bump won't be our only new resident soon. She's expecting kittens. Quite a few, I'd say."

A few days after Bump's arrival, Daisy, Charlie, Meirah and Mike received invitations to Kirsty and Cam's wedding.

"It's lovely of them to ask us," said Mike. "We're not even real relations."

"I know, Mike, but that's Kirsty all over, and I know she wants you both to be there," said Charlie. "How are we going to get round this other complication, though? I don't need to be here all the time, but the place can't run without you, Daisy."

"I'll just have to stay here then, Charlie."

Daisy tried to sound upbeat, but she was so disappointed. When Kirsty had first mentioned it to her, months ago now, there hadn't been a problem. She'd always have been able to find a stand-in in Blackheath. But now there was the business to consider.

"As long as we don't have any boarders — and even that would probably be okay with Belinda here to back me up — I can walk the daycare dogs, and Oscar can stay in the big house with us," Mike said.

"Don't be silly. You and Mummy have been invited as well."

"There's one small thing you've forgotten, Daisy," said Meirah. "Or possibly it's never even been mentioned before, I'm not sure."

"And that would be?"

Meirah shifted uncomfortably. "My phobia. Why do you think your father and I never go abroad for our holidays, except for that cruise when we sailed out of Southampton? I'm terrified of flying."

"I didn't know that."

"I don't suppose it's ever come up before. Much as I'd love to be there, nobody is going to get me up in one of those metal contraptions."

Daisy didn't know if there was any truth in what she'd just been told, but she knew her mother would do almost anything to make her happy.

"So what do you think, Daisy? We're more than happy to keep the place ticking over while you're away."

"With all that walking, you should have shed at least half a stone by the time we get back," said Daisy with a laugh. "And you realise you've opened the door to me going on holiday whenever I like if you're so willing to take over, don't you?"

"Shall I book the tickets then, Daisy?" said Charlie. "Do you have a passport? Oh, and you'll need a visa."

"Please, Charlie, and yes, I do have a passport. You all leave me with nothing to say and, even better, nothing to do. Thank you."

The following weekend, Jason came to visit Home Farm. It was one of those cold, crisp days where the sun shone brightly out of a gloriously blue sky. Daisy made lunch, then she and Jason wandered down to the stream and were watching the water trickle past their feet. There was a long pause in the conversation, and Daisy became aware of a change in the atmosphere. Jason was no longer relaxed.

"There's something I have to tell you, Daisy."

"Yes, I know. You're gay," she said, trying to lighten things up a bit.

"You know!"

"Oh my God, no! Of course I didn't know. I was joking. It's just, well, you never kissed me."

"It isn't a joke, Daisy."

"The kisses on the nose, on the cheek, the friendly hugs. I thought it was because you didn't fancy me."

"That bit's true. I'm sorry."

"No, please don't be sorry. I can't tell you how relieved I am. You've come to mean such a lot to me, Jason, but as a friend. Now you've told me this, we can still be friends. We don't have to split up and never see each other again."

"I'd like that. I wasn't sure you'd understand."

"Of course I do. Why are you telling me now?"

"'I'd have to have told you soon anyway. I've been feeling guilty for ages, thinking I was being deceitful, which I suppose I have been. But things have come to a head. I've met someone. For logistical reasons, the only day we can see each other is a Sunday. We've been meeting in the evenings during the week, but it isn't enough anymore. So…"

"You and I can meet up any time. It doesn't have to be a Sunday. It doesn't even have to be at the weekend. I can meet you in town after work, occasionally, if…" She looked questioningly at him.

"Rupert. His name's Rupert."

"…if Rupert doesn't mind you seeing me, that is."

"Of course he doesn't mind. He's been so worried you'd be upset that he nearly came with me. I told him I didn't think that would be a good idea."

Daisy was grateful. Somehow she didn't think that would have worked quite so well. Jason looked at his watch.

"You want to go now? You're meeting him?"

"If that's okay."

"Of course it is. Come on, I'll walk you back to your car. We can talk on the phone and arrange to meet up soon. And, Jason, I wish you all the luck and all the love in the world."

They hugged, he kissed her on the nose, and she watched him drive away. She was happy for him. What's more, she was happy for herself.

CHAPTER THIRTY-ONE

A few days before Kirsty's wedding, Daisy and Charlie were sitting on a plane bound for Hong Kong. They'd decided, in light of Meirah and Mike's generosity, to take an extra couple of days for a stopover. Neither had been there before.

Despite the luxury of travelling in business class on account of Charlie having long legs, they were in close proximity for many hours. They had not been so near each other since the time Daisy was ill and Charlie had moved into the flat to look after her. Daisy tried reading a book, but it didn't hold her attention. Watching a film about unrequited love served her no better, and when all was resolved at the end she could only wish for something she knew could never be.

"You're crying!" Charlie exclaimed.

"It's the film. They always have that effect on me."

He took the hankie from her hand and wiped away her tears. Later, when she slid past him to stretch her legs in the aisle, she stumbled because her knees were shaking so much and he grabbed hold of her to stop her falling. She tumbled onto his lap. They tried to brush it off, making a joke, but it had shaken both of them.

After a long, awkward journey, they were relieved to arrive in Hong Kong.

"I thought London was a busy city," said Charlie. "This is amazing!"

"How on earth do they get so many people in one place at the same time, Charlie? You can barely walk along the pavement without bumping into someone. For goodness' sake don't lose me," Daisy urged. "I wouldn't have a clue where to go."

Charlie pulled her arm through his own. "Just hang on to me. You'll be all right."

He'd forgotten about his vow to keep his distance. Even that simple contact made him ache for more. But she was right — because of the crowd, there was a danger they would get separated. Both were more aware of their touching than their surroundings. He tried for commonplace conversation.

"Just look at those skyscrapers!"

"I love it. I love all the bustle and the busyness. I don't think I could live here, though."

"No, and I now know I prefer living in the country anyway." What he really meant was that he preferred living in the country with Daisy.

"We must be getting old."

"It isn't that. I like the peace."

"Yeah, particularly when Oscar starts barking."

"You know what I mean."

"Yes, actually I do."

They took the tram to Victoria Peak and were rewarded with some amazing sights, including eagles flying beneath them as they ate lunch in one of the restaurants.

"Look at this, Charlie. This is the view I've seen in pictures. They must take the photos from this platform."

"You can understand why, can't you? What are you doing back there, anyway? You can see much more from here."

Charlie was standing close to the edge of the platform, but Daisy was maintaining a discreet distance. She remembered Kirsty's fear when they'd been on the London Eye and now felt a certain amount of sympathy. Charlie saw her hesitate.

"Here, give me your hand. I'll look after you."

He drew her towards him and stood behind her, his arms around her and his hands on the rail in front. They gazed at the panorama, lost in the moment, lost in each other. Each had the same thought. *My heart is breaking.*

They were glad they'd made the whirlwind trip, and neither would ever forget it, but both were relieved when it came to an end. They could focus on the next few days, and their excitement mounted as they boarded the plane for Melbourne. They'd forgotten about the exquisite torture of the journey, during which they were once again close together again for hours.

"You've shown me something of your hometown, Daisy. We've seen something quite different in Hong Kong. Now I'll be able to show you mine."

The wedding was due to take place two days after they arrived. Gilian picked them up from the airport and drove them to their hotel.

"Mum and Dad send their love," said Daisy. "They were so sorry they couldn't come, Gillian."

"It's okay, we understand. Meirah told me about her fear of flying. I'm terrified of heights, so I appreciate how she feels."

"You talk to her on the phone?"

"Often. We'll stay in touch, Daisy, even though I'm here."

"You're staying, then?"

"I am. I enjoyed my trip to England and I hope to make many more, but this is my home. My reason for going in the first place was you, and the rewards from that are more than I could ever have hoped for. I wanted to reunite you with James, and instead I found a whole new family for myself."

The next day, they were all gathered in Kirsty's flat. Cam and Charlie were discussing some last-minute details and Kirsty dragged Daisy to show her the dress, taking Gillian with them.

"Kirsty, it's beautiful. I can't wait to see you in it."

"Me neither," she giggled. "Cam's going to stay with his parents tonight, and Mum will be here, won't you, Mum?"

"Try keeping me away."

"Do you want to stay as well? We can squeeze you in. Then we can all get dressed and go together, unless you'd rather stay at the hotel and come with Charlie."

"Well, if it's okay, I'd love to stay here with you."

"Wonderful! Is your dress okay? How did it travel? You did say it was the one you wore to Sam and Niall's, didn't you?"

"Yes, I hope you don't mind."

"Mind! You looked beautiful in it. Gosh, I'm so excited."

"Shall I go back to the hotel now and collect my stuff?"

"My car's outside," said Gillian. "I'll drive you. You staying here, Kirsty?"

"Yes, Mum. See you in a bit."

Daisy and Gillian arrived back at the flat to find Kirsty and Charlie in the middle of what was obviously a tense conversation.

"You mean he's here, in Oz?" Charlie demanded.

"Yes, Charlie. If you remember, it wasn't his idea to go to the UK in the first place. He said there's nothing there for him anymore. Sorry, Daisy," Kirsty said as she noticed her sister come in, "and he's come home."

"And he wants to walk you down the aisle tomorrow?"

"Yes."

"And how do you feel about that?"

"I don't know, Charlie. It's not what I want, but I don't know what to do. He is my father, after all."

"But he isn't *my* father, and I'm the one who's supposed to be giving you away."

Daisy shot a startled look at Charlie. "Not your father?"

Charlie was far too angry and absorbed in the conversation to appreciate the significance of Daisy's question. He answered curtly. "Of course not. Whatever gave you that impression?"

For only the second time in her life, Daisy fainted.

When she came round, Daisy was lying on Kirsty's bed, and Charlie was sitting next to her, chafing her hand. There was no one else in the room. Charlie looked worried and hopeful at the same time.

"How do you feel? Are you okay?"

"It was a bit of a shock, that's all. I'll be fine. What did you mean in there?"

"Exactly what you think I meant. I had no idea you didn't know. My dad was killed in a car crash before I was born. James married Mum — or not, as we now know — and he adopted me. That's why we have the same surname." Charlie threw all caution to the wind. "I thought you wanted a brother. All these months, you've no idea the agony I've been in."

"But you never told me. I remember what you said to me the first time we met. 'I hope you're easier to get on with than my other sister,' you said. Other sister, Charlie. Not sister."

"Did you feel it too, right from the beginning?"

She didn't answer. She didn't need to.

"Daisy, are you feeling well enough to sit up yet?"

"I think so."

"Then I think it's time we put this relationship onto a proper footing, don't you?"

"I'd like that, Charlie. I'd like that very much."

When Daisy returned to the main room, Kirsty was on the phone to her father. They were both speaking loudly, so Daisy could hear both sides of the conversation.

"I don't want you to come to the wedding," said Kirsty. "In fact, I don't want to see you again. If you couldn't be bothered to get on a plane when I was at death's door, I don't see why you would want to give me away at my wedding."

"But Kirsty, I'm your father. It's my right."

"You gave up any rights you had long ago. You may not have deserted me as you did Daisy, but you might as well have. You never showed me any affection. In fact, I wish you had left me. I'd have been under no illusions then, not that I have been for a long time now. Leave it, Dad. Just leave it."

"I'm sorry you feel like that. I wish things were different."

He sounded sincere, but Kirsty knew that behind it all was the fact that he still needed Gillian's financial support. Everything he did was to serve himself.

"I wish you happy. You know that."

"Goodbye, Dad. Please don't call me again."

Kirsty burst into tears and Charlie wrapped her in his arms. She cried herself out and felt the better for it. "You've always looked after me, Charlie. Please will you give me away tomorrow?" she murmured.

"It was never in doubt as far as I'm concerned. I'm off now. I'll leave you three girls to talk about whatever it is girls talk about. I'll be here with the wedding car in the morning at eleven o'clock. Try and be ready," he said, blowing them all a kiss as he left.

Later, as the three women tucked into a takeaway, they discussed the events of the past year.

"I can't believe you didn't know that Charlie isn't James's son," said Gillian. "I can see why now, of course, but I suppose we just took it for granted that you did. We could all see how Charlie felt about you, but these things aren't always two-way, are they? We all thought you saw him only as a brother."

"What else could I do? As far as I was aware, that was exactly what he was."

"You must have been so unhappy all these months."

"You have no idea! Unhappy and at the same time content, because I'd found someone I felt so comfortable with."

"Comfortable?"

"Yes, I know it sounds daft, but in spite of everything we had such a lot of fun, such a lot in common. I had to try and make myself believe Charlie was my best friend."

"You were so brave to go ahead with the business."

"It was my dream, Gillian. And it was also my dream to be with Charlie. I thought I could cope. It's funny, you know," Daisy said, looking at Kirsty. "When we first met, Charlie threw me all those lavish compliments and you were so indignant. I was convinced it was because I was new and he was just being kind to me."

"Whereas I knew that he was flirting outrageously."

"I picked up on that pretty quickly too," Gillian said. "I admired his courage in going into this venture with you, as I now do yours. He's always been an equal partner in my own business. Somehow, though, he always saw it as mine. He's been so excited about Shepherds, at being in at the beginning of something."

"I suppose that was another red herring, wasn't it, the fact that you had the same surname?"

"Yes, Kirsty. It would never have occurred to me that James had adopted Charlie."

"Back then, when the children were small, he was still making some effort to be seen to be doing the right thing. I suppose I'll have to keep giving him an allowance. Much as it goes against my better judgement, I'm fairly sure he's incapable of making his way on his own. This time, I'll make it official. If there's a legal arrangement in place, I won't have to have anything to do with him ever again."

As Charlie handed his sister over to her groom the following morning, he glanced at Daisy, standing behind the bride and holding her bouquet, once more the bridesmaid. The look of love she gave him was beyond anything he could have hoped for in the previous months. He stepped back as the service began, knowing that the next wedding he went to would be his own and Daisy's.

At the reception, he related one or two anecdotes about his sister without embarrassing her. That was for the groom and the best man. He finished with a toast. "I'd like you all to raise your glasses to my once scruffy little sister who has turned into a beautiful swan. To Kirsty."

"To Kirsty!" everyone echoed.

CHAPTER THIRTY-TWO

There were no tears as Daisy and Charlie left for England. Everyone knew they would soon be together again. As members of the family assembled in the terminal building, Charlie had declared that he'd waited for long enough, and the sooner their own wedding could be arranged, the better.

Daisy entered a caveat. "I know we share a surname, Charlie, but I'm no longer prepared to be known as Daisy Shepherd. I'd like something new."

Back in England, Daisy and Charlie were picked up from the airport by Meirah and Mike, who knew nothing about the turn of events, secrecy having been imposed on the Australian side of the family.

"We saw some of the photos," said Meirah. "You'd never believe Kirsty had been so ill. She looked absolutely radiant."

"She was, Meirah. As was her sister," said Charlie. "In fact, she looked so beautiful I asked her to marry me."

Meirah was so astonished she stopped in her tracks and was almost mown down by someone pushing a baggage trolley. It took some minutes before they were able to make her and Mike understand the situation.

"I'd quite like to go home now, if that's okay," Daisy said. "It's been a long journey."

A while later, Daisy and Charlie were sitting side by side on the sofa with Oscar's chin wedged firmly between them.

"Nightcap?" Charlie offered.

"Actually I'd love a cup of tea."

"Coming right up." Charlie's vacated seat was immediately occupied by their canine companion. "We shouldn't really let him do that, should we?"

"Would you like to be the one to stop him? After all, you're the one who taught him to walk without pulling on his lead."

Charlie grinned ruefully. He liked having Oscar sitting next to him.

Daisy scratched behind the dog's ear and he thumped his tail in appreciation. Charlie came back with the tea and squidged Oscar along so that all three were sitting together. Daisy and Charlie held hands across his back while they drunk their tea. He didn't seem to mind.

"Time for bed, I think," said Charlie. "It'll take us a while to get back in sync after travelling halfway round the world."

This was the moment Daisy had been dreading. They hadn't been truly alone together since the wedding. The colour drained from her face, and he would have to have been completely insensitive not to notice. He raised the hand he was holding to his lips.

"Don't look so startled, Daisy. We've a lot of adjusting to do. It's going to be hard living under the same roof and sleeping in separate rooms, but that's exactly what we are going to do until the wedding. I've wanted you almost from the first moment we met, so I guess I can wait a while longer."

"I hoped... I didn't..."

"I get to have Oscar in my room, though."

Daisy picked up one of the scatter cushions and flung it at him.

Daisy and Charlie's wedding was arranged with almost as much unseemly haste as Sam and Niall's. Meirah accompanied her to the dress fitting and offered a few outrageous ideas.

"Are you serious, Mum?" Daisy laughed. "It's beautiful, but there's no way I'm going to be married in a Demis Roussos-type kaftan, colourful though it might be."

She chose an ivory charmeuse dress, deceptively simple with long sleeves and a full skirt. An Alice band would hold her curls in check, adorned with false diamonds and sapphires. They brought out the colour of her eyes and would be her 'something blue'.

Soon after their return from Australia, Charlie had taken her to a small but very stylish restaurant that Mike had recommended. By prior arrangement with the maître d', white chocolate truffles, one of Daisy's favourites, had been served with their coffee at the end of the meal. Five mouth-watering temptations sat in a circle, with a sixth in the centre, into which the sapphire engagement ring had been pushed. Removing any stickiness by wiping it on his napkin, Charlie vacated his chair and went down on one knee beside Daisy, sliding the ring onto her finger.

"I love you, Daisy Shepherd. Will you do me the very great honour of becoming my wife?"

Tears tumbled down her cheeks as she gasped, "Yes, Charlie. Oh, yes."

Applause broke out from the rest of the diners. Charlie rose to his feet, faced the onlookers and lifted his glass from the table. "Did you hear that? She said yes. I'm the happiest man alive. To Daisy."

"To Daisy!" came the resounding response.

Just over a week before the wedding, Gillian, Kirsty and Cam arrived from Australia. Back at Home Farm, Daisy took Kirsty back to the bungalow so they could spend some time alone.

"I'm dying to see your dress, Daisy."

"I'm dying to see yours too. Did it work out okay?"

"It's beautiful. I can't thank you enough for sending me the material so I could have it made up myself. It's travelled well too."

"Well, I certainly wasn't going to ask you and Sam to wear the same style. You're completely different heights, shapes and sizes, and what suits one of you wouldn't necessarily suit the other. I did want you to be in the same colour, though."

"It's the most amazing blue, almost alive."

"There was no way I was ever going to choose any other colour. It's my favourite, and it matches my engagement ring! Have I shown it to you?"

"Only about twenty times in the short while I've been here. I'll say one thing for my brother — he's got good taste."

"Is it strange for you? You have a sister on one side and a brother on the other, and they're getting married!"

"Off the scale, but I love it. Can't you just see the potential for outrageous conversation? 'Oh yes, my brother's married to my sister.' I can't wait to try it out."

"Not long now before you can. Only a week. I can't believe it."

The next day it had been arranged that they would all go to the church for a rehearsal. Sam and Niall had left the babies with her mother and various others had been invited — "to give it the right atmosphere," Mike had said mysteriously. "And though Daisy, Kirsty and Sam won't be wearing their proper dresses, it might be nice if we all get a bit poshed up."

There was only one person who was in on Mike and Meirah's little secret, and that was Gillian. She was the one person in contact with James. Now that he'd been run to ground, so to speak, Mike could fulfil his own long-held dream. Unknown to the rest, Meirah had at last been able to divorce James. He'd raised no objection. How could he? He was still reliant on Gillian financially, and that was one applecart he didn't want to upset. What everyone had thought was to be a rehearsal turned out to be a real wedding, just with a different couple. The brightly coloured kaftan Meirah had pretended to choose for Daisy was in fact for herself.

"It's a bit late for me to be wearing white, but I wanted to make sure you liked the dress," Meirah told her astonished daughter. "Even I'm not scatty enough to think it would have been right for your wedding, but it suits me down to the ground. I may even do a self-portrait."

Meirah did indeed look magnificent, and for once there wasn't a spot of paint on her. Mike looked adoringly at her, finally able to commit legally to the only woman who had ever held his heart.

CHAPTER THIRTY-THREE

The day of Daisy and Charlie's wedding dawned bright and sunny, and Daisy had a spot on her chin.

"Oh no! Why did this have to happen today of all days?"

Daisy was practically in tears as she called Kirsty into the bathroom to have a look. The groom was in the big house while the two sisters had stayed in the bungalow.

"Don't panic. I've seen make-up artists perform miracles," said Kirsty. "Once she's done with you, no-one will ever know."

Daisy made a little keening sound and Oscar came into the bathroom to see what was wrong just as the doorbell rang. Kirsty went to answer it, the dog nearly knocking her over in his rush to see who was there. It was Charlie.

"I thought I'd better ring. It's supposed to be unlucky to see the bride before the wedding, and I know what Daisy's like. You ready, Oscar?"

The dog demonstrated his eagerness by placing two large paws on his hero's shoulders.

"Good boy. Yes, I know. Come on then. Let's go for a walk and get out of the girls' way."

"Have they gone?" Daisy asked, peering round the edge of the bathroom door.

"Yes. You're safe to come out now, and Sam will be here with the hairdresser and the beautician in an hour, so you'd better have a shower and I'll make you some breakfast."

When everyone was ready, the cars arrived to take them to the old church in the village, a quintessentially English setting enhanced by a gloriously sunny day. Mike travelled with Daisy in one vintage Rolls Royce, preceded by another carrying Meirah, Gillian, Kirsty and Sam. With everyone in their place, Mike took his daughter's hand and placed it on his arm.

"You've never looked more beautiful, Daisy. I'm so proud of you. Charlie is a great man, and I know you're both going to be very happy."

They moved along the yew-lined path through the massive wooden doors and into the church. Daisy's heart was full to bursting when she saw all her Blackheath friends sitting in the pews as she and her father walked down the aisle. The only absentees were Gloria and Arnold, who had remained in America.

"It would break my heart to have to leave Oscar again, you see," Gloria had told Daisy on the phone. Daisy understood completely.

Further along Niall sat with two very well-behaved babies, ready for a quick exit should it be necessary. Aileen and Fergal were there too, having flown from Ireland specially, and next to them were Sam's parents. Even Jason was there with Rupert.

Daisy looked ahead to see Charlie, half-turned towards her, Cam at his side. The best man stepped back as Mike handed his daughter into Charlie's care and the couple turned to face the vicar to take their vows. When the vicar turned to Cam to ask for the rings, he bent down for a moment. Sitting at his side was a for once calm Oscar, and attached to his collar was a small velvet-covered box. It was removed and the pledges handed over. Daisy and Charlie had both wanted him to be present at the wedding. He had, after all, been there from the beginning.

The vicar took their hands, laying Daisy's on top of Charlie's, and spoke those immortal words: "I now pronounce you husband and wife. You may kiss the bride."

A NOTE TO THE READER

Dear Reader

I hope you have enjoyed *A Walk in the Park*. If you would consider leaving a review on **Amazon** or **Goodreads**, it would be much appreciated, though I would be just as happy if you'd like to join me on my **Facebook author page** for a chat. You can also visit me on **Twitter**, **Instagram** and my **website**.

Natalie

nataliekleinman.com

Sapere Books is an exciting new publisher of brilliant fiction and popular history.

To find out more about our latest releases and our monthly bargain books visit our website:
saperebooks.com

www.ingramcontent.com/pod-product-compliance
Lightning Source LLC
Chambersburg PA
CBHW060424180626
46817CB00007B/2658